Praise for Pastor Stephen G

MW01135695

"In this 11th installment of a thriller series, a combat-trained pastor helps protect a Chinese golfer and his cleric father... when the action does hit, it's exhilarating, and Stephen proves once again he's as capable in fights as he is in quieter times of prayer and worship. A fast-paced, exuberant outing for the virtuoso clergyman and his numerous comrades."

- Kirkus Reviews on *Deep Rough*

"Keating has accumulated an impressive assortment of characters in his series, and he gives each of them ample opportunity to shine... As in the preceding novels, the author skillfully blends Grant's sermonizing with intermittent bouts of violence. It creates a rousing moral quandary for readers to ponder without either side overwhelming the storyline. Tight action scenes complement the suspense (uncertainty over when the next possible attack will be) ... The villains, meanwhile, are just as rich and engrossing as the good guys and gals. The familiar protagonist, along with sensational new and recurring characters, drives an energetic political tale."

- Kirkus Reviews on *Reagan Country*

"It was my great privilege that Ronald Reagan and I were good friends and political allies. This exciting political thriller may be a novel but it truly captures President Reagan's optimism and principles."

- Ambassador Fred J. Eckert on *Reagan Country*

"First-rate supporting characters complement the sprightly pastor, who remains impeccable in this thriller."

- Kirkus Reviews on *Lionhearts*

"A first-rate mystery makes this a series standout..."

- Kirkus Reviews on Wine Into Water

"Ray Keating has created a fascinating and unique character in Pastor Grant. The way Keating intertwines politics, national security and faith into a compelling thriller is sheer delight."

- Larry Kudlow
formerly CNBC's *The Kudlow Report* and
current director of the National Economic Council

"The author packs a lot into this frantically paced novel... a raft of action sequences and baseball games are thrown into the mix. The multiple villains and twists raise the stakes... Stephen remains an engaging and multifaceted character: he may still use, when necessary, the violence associated with his former professions, but he at least acknowledges his shortcomings – and prays about it. Action fans will find plenty to love here, from gunfights and murder sprees to moral dilemmas."

- Kirkus Reviews on Murderer's Row

Murderer's Row was named KFUO's BookTalk "Book of the Year" in 2015.

"It's kind of a cool book. If you like Tom Clancy, if you like action, if you like some nail-biting stuff, this is it."

- The Rev. Kenneth V. Blanchard,
"Black Man with a Gun" Podcast,
on *Deep Rough*

The River was a 2014 finalist for KFUO's BookTalk "Book of the Year."

"Ray Keating is a great novelist."

"A gritty, action-stuffed, well-considered thriller with a gun-toting clergyman."

"President Ronald Reagan's legacy will live on in the U.S., around the world and in the pages of history. And now, thanks to Ray Keating's *Reagan Country*, it will live on in the world of fiction. *Reagan Country* ranks as a page-turning thriller that pays homage to the greatest president of the twentieth century."

"Mr. Keating's storytelling is so lifelike that I almost thought I had worked with him when I was at Langley. Like the fictitious pastor, I actually spent 20 years working for the U.S. intelligence community, and once I started reading *The River*, I had to keep reading because it was so well-crafted and easy to follow and because it depicted a personal struggle that I knew all too well. I simply could not put it down."

"I miss Tom Clancy. Keating fills that void for me."

Marvin Olasky, editor-in-chief of WORLD magazine, lists Ray Keating among his top 10 Christian novelists.

"Pastor Grant continues to be one of the most entertaining heroes in the political thrillers and suspense genre. With occasional pop-ins from fan-favorite recurring characters, *Deep Rough* fits in perfectly with the rest of the series – quirky, tightly woven, and difficult to put down. Keating manages to keep his writing fresh and surprising with every new Pastor Grant book. This series satisfies yet again, finding unique ways to entertain and enlighten along the way."

- Self-Publishing Review on *Deep Rough*

"Must read for any Reaganite."

- Craig Shirley,
Reagan biographer and presidential historian,
on Reagan Country

"Keating's creativity and storytelling ability remain on point, for a fun and different take on Pastor Grant, and one that's just as satisfying as longer books in the series."

- Self-Publishing Review on *Heroes and Villains*

"Ray Keating has a knack for writing on topics that could be pulled from tomorrow's headlines."

- Lutheran Book Review on
An Advent for Religious Liberty

"*Root of All Evil?* is an extraordinarily good read. Only Ray Keating could come up with a character like Pastor Stephen Grant."

- Paul L. Maier, author of A Skeleton in God's Closet, More Than A Skeleton, and The Constantine Codex

"Thriller and mystery writers have concocted all manner of main characters, from fly fishing lawyers to orchid aficionados and former ballplayers, but none has come up with anyone like Stephen Grant, the former Navy Seal and CIA assassin, and current Lutheran pastor. Grant mixes battling America's enemies and sparring with enemies of traditional Christian values, while ministering to his Long Island flock. The amazing thing is that the character works. The Stephen Grant novels are great reads beginning with *Warrior Monk*, which aptly describes Ray Keating's engaging hero."

- David Keene, former opinion editor at *The Washington Times*

"*Warrior Monk* by Ray Keating has all of the adventure, intrigue, and believable improbability of mainstream political thrillers, but with a lead character, Pastor Stephen Grant, that resists temptation."

- *Lutheran Book Review* on *Warrior Monk*

THE TRAITOR

A Pastor Stephen Grant Novel

RAY KEATING

All the best!

Ray Keating

This book is a work of fiction. Names, characters, places, events and incidents either are the product of the author's imagination or are used fictitiously. Any resemblance to actual persons, living or dead, events or locales is entirely coincidental.

For more information:
Keating Reports, LLC
raykeating@keatingreports.com

ISBN-13: 9781709209772

Cover design by Tyrel Bramwell.

*For
Beth,
Jonathan
and
Mikayla & David*

Previous Books by Ray Keating

Deep Rough: A Pastor Stephen Grant Novel (2019)

Warrior Monk: A Pastor Stephen Grant Novel
(Second Edition, 2019)

Shifting Sands: A Pastor Stephen Grant Short Story (2018)

Heroes & Villains: A Pastor Stephen Grant Short Story (2018)

Reagan Country: A Pastor Stephen Grant Novel (2018)

Lionhearts: A Pastor Stephen Grant Novel (2017)

Wine Into Water: A Pastor Stephen Grant Novel (2016)

Murderer's Row: A Pastor Stephen Grant Novel (2015)

The River: A Pastor Stephen Grant Novel (2014)

*An Advent for Religious Liberty:
A Pastor Stephen Grant Novel* (2012)

Root of All Evil? A Pastor Stephen Grant Novel (2012)

Warrior Monk: A Pastor Stephen Grant Novel (2010)

In the nonfiction arena...

The Disney Planner 2020: The TO DO List Solution (2019)

*Free Trade Rocks! 10 Points on International Trade Everyone
Should Know* (2019)

A Discussion Guide for Ray Keating's Warrior Monk
(Second Edition, 2019)

The Realistic Optimist TO DO List & Calendar 2019 (2018)

*Unleashing Small Business Through IP:
The Role of Intellectual Property in Driving Entrepreneurship,
Innovation and Investment* (Revised and Updated Edition, 2016)

*Unleashing Small Business Through IP:
Protecting Intellectual Property, Driving Entrepreneurship*
(2013)

*Discussion Guide for Warrior Monk:
A Pastor Stephen Grant Novel* (2011)

"Chuck" vs. the Business World: Business Tips on TV (2011)

U.S. by the Numbers:
What's Left, Right, and Wrong with America State by State
(2000)

New York by the Numbers:
State and City in Perpetual Crisis (1997)

D.C. by the Numbers: A State of Failure (1995)

"We ask you, brothers, to respect those who labor among you and are over you in the Lord and admonish you, and to esteem them very highly in love because of their work. Be at peace among yourselves. And we urge you, brothers, admonish the idle, encourage the fainthearted, help the weak, be patient with them all. See that no one repays anyone evil for evil, but always seek to do good to one another and to everyone. Rejoice always, pray without ceasing, give thanks in all circumstances; for this is the will of God in Christ Jesus for you."

- 1 Thessalonians 5:12-18

My shield is with God,
who saves the upright in heart.
God is a righteous judge,
and a God who feels indignation every day.
If a man does not repent, God will whet his sword;
he has bent and readied his bow;
he has prepared for him his deadly weapons,
making his arrows fiery shafts.
Behold, the wicked man conceives evil
and is pregnant with mischief
and gives birth to lies.
He makes a pit, digging it out,
and falls into the hole that he has made.
His mischief returns upon his own head,
and on his own skull his violence descends.
I will give to the Lord the thanks due to his righteousness,
and I will sing praise to the name of the Lord,
the Most High.

- Psalm 7:10-17

Brief Dossiers on Recurring Characters

Pastor Stephen Grant. After college, Grant joined the Navy, became a SEAL, and went on to work at the CIA. He subsequently became a Lutheran pastor, serving at St. Mary's Lutheran Church on the eastern end of Long Island. Grant grew up in Ohio, just outside of Cincinnati. He possesses a deep knowledge of theology, history, and weapons. His other interests include archery, golf, movies, the beach, poker and baseball, while also knowing his wines, champagnes and brews. Stephen Grant is married to Jennifer Grant.

Jennifer Grant. Jennifer is a respected, sought-after economist and author. Along with Yvonne Hudson and Joe McPhee, she is a partner in the consulting firm Coast-to-Coast Economics. Her first marriage to then-Congressman Ted Brees ended when the congressman had an affair with his chief of staff. Jennifer loves baseball (a Cardinals fan while her husband, Stephen, cheers on the Reds) and literature, and has an extensive sword and dagger collection. Jennifer grew up in the Las Vegas area, with her father being a casino owner.

Paige Caldwell. For part of Stephen Grant's time at the CIA, Paige Caldwell was his partner in the field and in the bedroom. After Stephen left the Agency, Paige continued with the CIA until she eventually was forced out. However, she went on to start her own firm, CDM International Strategies and Security, with two partners – Charlie Driessen and Sean McEnany.

Charlie Driessen. Charlie was a longtime CIA veteran, who had worked with both Stephen Grant and Paige Caldwell. Driessen left the Agency to work with Paige at CDM. Prior to the CIA, he spent a short time with the Pittsburgh police department.

Sean McEnany. After leaving the Army Rangers, Sean McEnany joined the security firm CorpSecQuest, which was part legitimate business and part CIA front. He later signed up with Caldwell and Driessen at CDM. He maintains close contact with the CIA, and has a secret, high-security office in the basement of his suburban Long Island home, along with a mobile unit disguised as a rather typical van parked in the driveway. McEnany's ability to obtain information across the globe has an almost mystical reputation in national security circles. For good measure, Sean, his wife, Rachel, and their children attend St. Mary's Lutheran Church, where Stephen Grant is pastor.

Chase Axelrod. Chase worked with Sean McEnany at CorpSecQuest, and then became an employee of CDM. He grew up in Detroit, became a star tight end with a 4.0 grade point average in college, and then earned a master's degree in foreign languages from N.C. State. He has mastered six foreign languages – Mandarin, German, French, Russian, Spanish and Japanese.

Father Tom Stone. A priest and rector at St. Bartholomew's Anglican Church on Long Island, Tom is one of Grant's closest friends, and served as Stephen's best man. He enjoyed surfing while growing up in southern California, and is known for an easygoing manner and robust sense of humor. Along with Stephen, Tom and two other friends regularly meet for morning devotions and conversation at a local diner, and often play golf together. Tom is married to Maggie Stone, who runs her own public relations business. They are the parents to six children.

Father Ron McDermott. Father McDermott is a priest at St. Luke's Roman Catholic Church and School. McDermott is part of the morning devotions group of friends at the diner. He is a strong and caring leader of the St. Luke's school.

Pastor Zackary Charmichael. Zack also is a pastor at St. Mary's Lutheran Church, and the most recent addition to the breakfast clergy club. He grew up in the state of Washington, is a comic-book and gaming nerd, and a big fan of Seattle's Mariners and Seahawks as well as Vancouver's Canucks. Zack also is Tom Stone's son-in-law, married to Tom's oldest daughter, Cara, who is a nurse.

Joan and George Kraus. Joan and George attend St. Mary's Lutheran Church, and are friends with Stephen and Jennifer, with Jennifer and Joan being particularly close, almost like sisters. Joan teaches math at a Long Island Lutheran high school, while George has his own law practice. They have two daughters – Grace and Faith.

Chapter 1

"It's kind of breathtaking," whispered Paige Caldwell, as she looked out at more than 500,000 citizens of Hong Kong gathered in and around Victoria Park.

Caldwell's comment was captured by a tiny, two-way communication device hidden in her right ear, and transmitted to three of her colleagues from CDM International Strategies and Security.

Chase Axelrod responded, "After President Bo Liang's death, they've gotten a whiff of freedom."

Charlie Driessen added, "Maybe they'll give us a statue next to Queen Victoria, or at least a nice thank you."

Through gritted teeth, Caldwell scolded, "Charlie."

"Yeah, yeah, sorry, but it's just us."

Sean McEnany chimed in, "Never assume anything."

Driessen grunted in response.

The four were in Hong Kong at the behest of the CIA. The Agency wanted to be close to Andy Faan, a leader in the Hong Kong pro-democracy movement, and turned to CDM to do the job. In fact, CDM was able to serve as private security for Faan in addition to protections that the pro-democracy groups were able to supply – which was, to say the least, limited.

Faan sat on a stage in a folding chair, alongside other speakers. These protestors were working together to oppose efforts by the mainland Chinese communist government to grab greater control over Hong Kong's political and legal systems, as well as its economy.

The CDM group was spread out around the stage, with each dressed to blend in with the crowd. The tools of their trade – Glocks and tactical knives all around – were well hidden from casual or even prying eyes, yet still easily accessible if needed.

The event approached the two-hour mark.

Driessen whispered, "I'm with these guys, but somebody needs to be ready with the hook when they go on too long. And each one, so far, has gone on too long."

McEnany replied, "Stop bitchin', Charlie. This is history."

Driessen grunted, once again. His sarcasm and sometimes indecipherable utterances kind of matched Driessen's look, which featured barely tamed but thinning hair, an unruly mustache, and rumpled clothing.

Caldwell added, "Putting aside Charlie's complaining, his point is a reminder that we've probably got another two hours before Faan takes the stage to close this thing out."

Axelrod was covering the area behind the stage and a large dark curtain. Backstage had been rather quiet since the event kicked off, while McEnany patrolled in front of the stage, and Caldwell watched from the left side and Driessen the right.

Some 90 minutes later, McEnany moved toward an area set aside for the media. He had passed by the group several times already, but in this instance, a correspondent with the Xinhua News Agency, an organ of the Chinese government, started to slip a phone into his jacket pocket, stepped forward, and bumped into McEnany. The phone fell to the ground, and the two men bent down to retrieve it. As they did so, the correspondent, Ping Ho, whispered, "The Ministry of State Security is going to arrest Faan after he speaks."

McEnany grabbed the phone. As they stood up, he handed it to Ho. McEnany merely said, "Excuse me."

Ho nodded.

The two men continued walking in different directions.

McEnany waited for the cover of crowd noise before relaying Ho's message to his team. "Not sure if you heard that, but I was told that the MSS is going to grab Faan after his speech. And before anyone asks, yes, this person would know and is reliable. I fully trust him."

Caldwell whispered, "Shit."

Axelrod reported, "They've got to know that he's supposed to leave from behind the stage. I'm not spotting anything signaling the MSS, at least not yet."

Driessen offhandedly added, "Apparently, the new Chinese president isn't all that different from the old one."

McEnany volunteered, "If they take Faan, no one's going to see him again. Plan B or C?" The muscular, five-foot-ten-inch McEnany continued his casual movements, including scratching the scalp underneath his short blond hair.

During their prep for the event, CDM had come up with two alternatives for extracting Faan if a situation like this developed. Plan B called for getting him out before he spoke, then to a CIA safehouse. Plan C was a post-speech strategy to move Faan off the stage and into the crowd, and in the confusion, lose whomever was after him. Again, the short-term destination would be the safehouse. When Caldwell informed Faan of the options on the previous night, he didn't seem too keen on either, offering no real response.

Axelrod said, "He's never going to go for B. He'll insist on speaking."

Caldwell said, "Yeah, you're right. Plan C presents all kinds of risks, but it's better than just letting the MSS arrest Faan." She paused, and then said, "Okay, I'll make my way to Faan and let him know the situation. After that, we'll move into place to move him when he's finished speaking."

She received affirmative responses, and made her way around the back of and then onto the stage. Caldwell's beauty usually shone through, including her black hair, steely blue eyes, full lips and freckles, but she was skilled in emphasizing it when needed, or as was the case now, limiting it with rather mundane, even drab attire. Few seemed to take note of her moving into an empty chair, and whispering into Andy Faan's ear. "We've received reliable information that the MSS is going to arrest you after your speech."

Faan turned his head, raised an eyebrow and looked into Caldwell's eyes. "You are sure?"

Caldwell nodded.

Faan said, "I am going to speak. I am not leaving."

"I understand. That means we'll need to go to Plan C."

Faan sighed, and remained silent.

At the microphone, the declarations by one of the pro-democracy speakers generated cheers among the crowd.

Caldwell asked, "Mr. Faan, Plan C?"

"I suppose we don't have a choice." He paused, and looked out at the hundreds of thousands of people gathered. The expression on his face changed. "Ms. Caldwell, be ready with Plan C. But perhaps I can get more people on our side by shedding some light on the current situation."

Caldwell stared at Faan. "Is that the best move?"

Faan replied, "I'm not saying this because I am the target, but this is a clear example of why we are gathered here today. The Chinese government wants to control our ability to speak out, and they want to make those who would disagree with them disappear."

Caldwell nodded. "I understand. I'm going to remain on the side of the stage, and will signal you if, or when, we spot the MSS people. My team will be ready for whatever happens."

"Thank you." He leaned in closer. "How did you come across this information?"

Caldwell paused. She answered, "A friend of ours and of freedom working in the Chinese state media."

Faan smiled. "A well-placed patriot. Please thank him, or her, for me."

"We will."

An hour later, as Andy Faan began to speak to the throng of people, three dark SUVs stopped some 60 yards away on one of the streets leading to the park. Two men exited from each vehicle, with the drivers remaining behind the respective wheels. All were dressed in black.

Axelrod spotted them immediately. He reached inside his jacket, felt the Glock and then checked his knife. Axelrod's skills with both were matched by his size and strength. His six-foot-three-inch body was capable of unleashing a fury well beyond what he used on the gridiron during college. He reported, "The MSS thugs have arrived."

Driessen said, "I hope Faan knows what he's doing."

Caldwell replied, "Me, too."

When Faan glanced in her direction, Caldwell nodded at him.

She whispered to the CDM group, "He knows."

Axelrod interrupted, "Crap."

"What is it?" replied Caldwell and McEnany at the same time.

"The MSS apparently has backup. Two troop transports just pulled up not far beyond the SUVs. The Chinese army is arriving."

Caldwell said, "Shit. We should have gotten Faan out of here while we could."

Driessen responded, "He wasn't going to let us take him anywhere."

Axelrod offered, "Well, at least I'm not seeing anything beyond the three SUVs and the two troop trucks."

Driessen asked, "Is that good news?"

McEnany speculated, "It might be. It tells me that they're not looking for a bloodbath ... hopefully."

"The troops haven't moved out of the trucks yet," reported Axelrod.

McEnany observed, "It's all up to Faan now."

About twenty minutes later, Faan had the massive crowd hanging on every word.

Driessen commented, "Geez, they love this guy."

"He's the real thing," commented McEnany in matter-of-fact fashion.

Faan lowered the microphone and took a deep breath. He then said, "Before we leave here today, I want to remove any doubts about what we are saying and why we are here. The mainland communist government does not like freedom, whether it be freedom of speech, religion or the press. That government does not seek to protect our natural rights, but instead, they seek to make government the creator and denier of rights."

Axelrod said, "Six MSS agents are moving forward."

Caldwell looked at the curtain hanging behind Faan. She said, "Chase, let's help Faan show what's happening."

Axelrod paused, and then said, "The curtain?"

"Yeah."

"I'm with you."

The two moved into place, while Faan continued speaking.

When Andy Faan finally said, "I have received what I consider to be accurate information that the Chinese Ministry of State Security is planning to arrest me when I finish speaking."

The six MSS agents had climbed the stairs and were waiting on the other side of the curtain. Hearing Faan's words, they froze.

Axelrod, who understood most of the Cantonese being spoken, said, "Now." Caldwell and Axelrod pulled open the large curtain, exposing the six MSS agents to hundreds of thousands of increasingly angry and outraged residents of Hong Kong.

Faan glanced behind him, turned back to the microphone, and said, "These apparently are the men sent to arrest me. But this is bigger than me, my friends, This is about all of us, and about basic human freedoms being crushed by an abusive regime."

Shouts of anger and calls for freedom rose up from the crowd.

Driessen said, "What the hell is going to happen?"

Each of the CDM personnel placed a hand on their gun. The MSS agents did the same. In the distance, the members of the People's Liberation Army started moving out of the troop transports.

But one of the MSS agents raised a hand to cover an earpiece in an apparent effort to hear more clearly as angry shouts grew louder from hundreds of thousands of people.

The six MSS agents suddenly turned, and moved rapidly down the stairs and away from the stage.

As they climbed back into the SUVs and the vehicles pulled away, followed by the troop transports, Faan led the crowd in a chant of "Freedom!"

Later that night, Sean McEnany sent an encrypted message to Ping Ho: "Thank you, once again, for your work and courage. The information you passed along saved Andy Faan and might have saved the pro-democracy, pro-freedom movement."

Ho responded, "I do what I must. I thank God for you and your friends. You are taking risks when you do not have to do so."

McEnany replied, "Stay strong, my friend, and God bless."

Chapter 2

One month later

This would be Hunter Bryant's last day at the Central Intelligence Agency, though none of his supervisors or colleagues were aware of this fact. The 28-year-old had been at the Agency for five years. His family background and education made gaining employment with the CIA as close to a slam dunk as possible. Bryant's father, now retired, had risen to colonel in the U.S. Army. His older brother served in the Navy, and Bryant's sister worked at the FBI. For good measure, his mother was a vice president with a defense contractor involved with providing parts and technical training to the Air Force.

While Bryant drifted through high school, his grades were solid and he never got into any serious trouble. And his time at college led to a degree in computer science and graduating near the top of his class.

It was all very Bryant-like when Hunter landed an IT job with the CIA, and his skills quickly put him to work as a specialist in protecting computer networks and online communications against all kinds of threats.

Hunter Bryant seemed to step right out of central casting for work at the CIA.

It was late on a Thursday afternoon, and Bryant was in one of the server rooms at Langley. This was typical.

What came next was anything but typical. After one of his co-workers left, Bryant was alone. He opened an access port on a server, and plugged in a smartphone. The CIA's Langley facility rated as a SCIF, that is, a Secure Compartmented Information Facility, so personal electronic devices were no-no's. This was an Agency device, though it didn't matter for Bryant's purposes.

He had written and installed a program on the phone. It downloaded an assortment of files from the server. He unplugged the device, and started to head back to his desk. While walking, Bryant slipped the phone into his shirt chest pocket. Inside the fabric of the pocket were sewn tiny, smart microdots. Once a device had been placed in the pocket, the three digital microdot devices were programmed to extend sharp arms to pierce the pocket fabric and attach themselves to the device. In seconds, the contents of the phone's memory and SIM card were copied, digitally stored on each high-capacity microdot, and then erased on the phone.

By the time Bryant arrived at his desk, the tiny devices' tasks had been completed. He removed the phone from his pocket and placed it on his desk.

After a casual conversation and a few "See you tomorrow" comments to co-workers, Hunter Bryant exited the New Headquarters Building at the George Bush Center for Intelligence, got in his car, and drove away from the facility grounds. No one was aware of the files that were stolen, and now were located inside the fabric of Hunter Bryant's shirt pocket.

Rather than driving to his apartment, he went straight to Dulles International Airport. By the time Bryant – traveling under a different name supported by flawless identification documents – was on his connecting flight in Europe, his preset email message about being sick and missing work would be delivered early on Friday morning.

Chapter 3

Seated at one end of a long pine dining room table, Stephen Grant looked at his wife, Jennifer, sitting at the opposite end, with some of their friends sprinkled on each side. Amidst the chatter, he took a mental breather just to watch his wife, who was so clearly enjoying this gathering. Stephen loved her smile, brown eyes, short auburn hair, sharp facial features but with a slightly upturned nose, and a voice and laugh that combined touches of refinement with seductiveness. But it was her energy, compassion and warmth that really pulled him in every time.

Stephen broke his mental gaze and said, "Okay, people, it's almost game time, and I promised Jennifer that I would handle the rest of the evening's food and beverage options. And what I mean by that is cleaning up dinner, putting out desserts for everyone to enjoy on their own schedule, and making sure drinks are full."

"Well, I'm impressed," commented Maggie Stone.

Stephen replied, "Thanks."

Maggie smiled, and said, "No, I was talking to Jennifer." She looked at Jennifer. "You have Stephen trained well. I can't get Tom to do anything like that."

"Hey!" protested Tom Stone.

Stephen added, "I think I should be insulted as well."

Tom Stone was one of Stephen's closest friends – including being best man at Stephen and Jennifer's wedding – and the priest and rector at St. Bartholomew's Anglican Church. He and Maggie had six children.

Ron McDermott, another of Stephen's good friends and a priest at St. Luke's Roman Catholic Church and School, commented, "It's not an insult. Jennifer and Maggie are simply making statements of fact about husbands who need, let's just say, guidance."

Tom smiled and countered, "If you were allowed to get married, now then we would have to pray for a woman and her suffering."

Jennifer said, "Now, now, boys, play nice."

Maggie added, "Do they ever, Jennifer?"

Joan and George Kraus also were at the table. Joan, a math teacher at a Lutheran high school, and Jennifer were as close as sisters. George had his own law firm, and was known for his conservatism in nearly all things, including his neatly cut brown hair and attire that usually involved a navy blazer. That made for an interesting complement to Joan's bright red hair, large blue eyes, and colorful fashion choices.

Joan asked, "Stephen, would you like some help?"

"No, thanks, Joan. Head into the living room and relax. I've got this under control."

Ron said, "Actually, I'll help Stephen, and I required no training to do so."

Ron's mannerisms, his look – a stocky, muscular five-foot-six-inch build with short blond hair – and a very dry sense of humor meant that it often took people some time to understand that he was a compassionate priest.

After the others made their way from the dining room into the living room, Stephen and Ron undertook the movement of dishes and utensils to the dishwasher, and packed up leftovers into containers and the refrigerator.

As they proceeded, Ron asked, "So, are you getting ready for the trip and retreat?"

"I'm getting closer to having church and schedule matters set. I've been working to get ahead on the things I can. Zack has been great, and the fact that I can tie in the trip with a couple of meetings for the Lutheran Response to Christian Persecution makes it easier to justify."

Ron shook his head. "You know, Stephen, you don't have to justify a retreat once in a while. You can just appreciate it."

Stephen stopped in mid-stride. "Yeah, I know. Sometimes I have a tough time doing that. For some reason, I feel guilty. I'm looking forward to this, and I appreciate you inviting me after Stan had to drop out."

The trip to a monastery in the French Alps was just over a month away. It was scheduled to last for two-and-a-half weeks. The monastery ran an almost year-round program of offering two to three week stays for members of the clergy – mainly, Roman Catholics, but a few non-Catholics sprinkled in, like Pastor Grant. The guests would not only gain time for rest removed from much of daily life, but also be offered set time for prayer; worship, from Matins to Vespers; some study; and hands on work in the monastery. That work mainly meant being involved with what the Monastere de Saint Paul had become known for across Europe and beyond – rich, delicious French chocolate.

Ron said, "Even though you're a Lutheran, you're going to love the Monastere de Saint Paul."

"You certainly had nothing but positive things to say about your visit a few years ago. By the way, there's at least one Lutheran monastery in the U.S., and I know of a few in Europe."

"What would Martin Luther say?"

"Perhaps we can discuss that on the trip."

"I think Luther would have a different take on the Monastere de Saint Paul if he had tasted their chocolate."

Stephen smiled, and said, "Yeah. Apparently, they're very well known, considering that Zack and Cara, Tom and Maggie, and Jen, all have requests in for me to bring back the monks' French chocolate."

Ron nodded, "It's very good, and I have numerous requests as well."

Jennifer entered the kitchen, and asked, "Are you talking about your trip?"

Stephen replied, "We are."

Jennifer said, "You know, Ron, the only reason I'm okay with this is the chocolate. Stephen pledged to bring home a variety of French chocolates from the monks."

Ron smiled, and commented, "Jennifer, what's not to like? You get rid of this guy for a few weeks, and then he'll return with some of the best chocolates from Europe."

Jennifer laughed, followed the two into the dining room, looked at what had been laid out, and said, "Looks like you've got everything covered. Thanks."

Ron and Stephen both said, "You're welcome."

Jennifer added, "Let's go watch the game. The Cardinals just took the lead. Molina hit a two-run homer."

Chapter 4

Sonja Iglesias arrived at her desk at Langley before seven in the morning. While first sitting down, she knocked over her iced vanilla latte. The cap remained on the cup, so only small amounts of the coffee-and-milk beverage escaped onto her desk. Iglesias' cursing in response to the accident, however, made it clear that she was displeased with the start of her Friday.

As she began scrolling through email on her desktop, frustration apparently lingered as she deleted items with overly zealous striking of the "delete" key.

She stopped to read the email from Hunter Bryant. No one was in the vicinity, but Iglesias spoke out loud anyway. "Really! Why can't these people follow simple instructions on sick days?" She sighed. "And stomach issues strike on a Friday? How original."

Iglesias proceeded to call Bryant's Agency-issued cellphone, personal cell, and land line. In each case, she left basically the same message: "Hunter, I received your email, and I'm sorry that you're not feeling well. But you know that procedures for sick days suggest calling and talking to me or leaving a message. Of course, if you're unable to do so, I understand, but we've put these procedures in effect for substantive reasons. So, just give me a quick call. Thanks."

After another hour passed, Iglesias received an email from another member of her team saying that she, too, wouldn't be making it into work due to stomach problems.

Iglesias, once again, spoke to no one in particular. "Oh, come on."

She called that person as well. The employee answered, and managed to apologize between retching sounds. After the call ended, Iglesias drummed her fingers on the desk. She repeated the same three calls to Bryant as earlier. Again, there was no answer, but she didn't leave messages this time.

Iglesias rose from her chair, walked over to the doorway of her office, and looked out at a bullpen area. She spotted Clifford Hayden at his station.

As she approached, Hayden said, "Good morning, boss."

"Morning, Cliff."

"Something I can do for you?"

"Indulge me. I managed little sleep last night, and the start of my Friday hasn't exactly been ideal."

"Sorry to hear that."

"Between you and me, part of my frustration this morning is people not following simple policies, like calling in when sick rather than sending an email or a text."

"Gotcha."

"So, again, indulge me by tracking down where Bryant's Agency cell is right now."

"Hunter's?"

"Yes."

Hayden shook his head and smiled. "He's sick, but he emailed you instead of calling. Not surprised. He's one of those guys who would rather text or email than actually talk to someone on the phone." He started pecking away at his keyboard, while turning to look at the screen. "Sure, give me a second. If it's on, I'll have it in a few seconds. If it's off, then I can, as you know, turn it on and then tell you where it is. That'll add a minute or two to the process."

Iglesias watched the screen as well with her arms folded, with one finger tapping her bicep.

Hayden reported, "It's not on." He continued working away, while Iglesias' finger kept tapping.

"I believe I've got it..." His voice trailed off. "And here we go. Oh."

"What's 'oh'?" asked Iglesias.

"The phone is at Dulles." He clicked more keys. "Yeah. It's in a parking lot at Dulles."

Iglesias leaned down, placing one hand on Hayden's desk and the other on the back of his chair. She looked at the map on the screen. "What the hell?"

Hayden remained silent.

Iglesias asked him, "Do you have a lot of shit this morning?"

"A fair amount."

"Well, put it aside. Your new assignment is to find out where Hunter flew off to and when."

Just over an hour later, Hayden knocked on Iglesias' open office door.

She said, "Yes, come in."

Hayden did so, and closed the door behind him.

Iglesias continued, "So, where the fuck did Bryant fly to while being so sick?"

Hayden shrugged his shoulders. "I have no idea. I cannot find an airline ticket for Hunter Bryant anywhere."

"What?"

Hayden shook his head. "Nothing."

"Shit. I don't like this."

"I figured you wouldn't."

Iglesias sat down at her desk, and resumed drumming her fingers. She looked up at Hayden. "Okay, set up shop over there." She pointed to her own computer station in the office. "I want a video rundown on what Bryant was doing around here yesterday. And I want to know where the hell he is right now."

Twenty minutes later, Hayden said, "You need to see this."

The two watched the video of Hunter Bryant in the server room on the previous day's afternoon, plugging a smartphone into a server.

Sonja Iglesias said, "That little shit."

Chapter 5

While Sonja Iglesias and Cliff Hayden were delving deeper into what their colleague had done, two massive, square-jawed security men led Hunter Bryant into the vast, wood-paneled office of Garth Bellanger. The security duo's dark shirts and suits seemed to be barely succeeding in an effort to constrain the men's sculpted muscles.

Bellanger looked up from his desk, and smiled broadly. He rose and declared, "Hunter, I am so glad to see you are here safe and sound."

Garth Bellanger was a mid-sixties Frenchman who had made a fortune at the fringes of the computer and telecommunications revolutions over the past four-plus decades. He dressed like a Steve Jobs wannabe – sneakers, jeans and t-shirt. Rather than black, though, Bellanger's shirt was always forest green. Bellanger also chose for his long, thin head to be completely clean shaven.

Rather than being an innovator, however, Bellanger was adept at stealing intellectual property, and more. In recent years, he had increased his bank account and raised his public profile by taking information from companies and countries around the world. Some of that information would be sold to those who valued it greatly. Indeed, Bellanger often would be hired to acquire specific information. Other information, though, had limited black market value, usually being more political in nature. Such information would be used by Bellanger – that is, released publicly – to inflict damage on those who irritated or bothered him in some way. When doing so, Garth Bellanger professed to be acting according to high principles, claiming the vaunted mantle of exposing government secrets. A hodgepodge of Leftists, Marxists, populists, anarchists, isolationists, Luddites, and hyper-libertarians praised his work as heroic. Bellanger stepped out from behind his desk, and while starting to cover the substantial space in the room, he opened his arms wide. When the two men finally met in the middle of the office, they embraced. Bellanger then enthusiastically kissed Bryant on each cheek.

"It's good to see you, Garth," said Bryant. "It's kind of a relief to be here with you." Bellanger's estate was a few miles outside of Paris.

"Don't be merely relieved, my dear friend. Instead, be pleased with what you have accomplished. This will be a time of celebration."

Bellanger looked at the two men who accompanied Bryant, and ordered, "Gentlemen, you may leave, and please send in Dr. Rossi."

They both responded, "Yes, sir."

Bellanger put an arm around Bryant's shoulders, and steered him in the direction of his ornate desk. They exchanged niceties about Bryant's flight, and Bellanger spoke of the suite prepared for Bryant and the dinner they would enjoy.

Bellanger said, "Please, take a seat."

As Bryant slumped a bit in the high-backed chair, the door at the far end of the room re-opened. The sound of the door opening and closing was followed by the rapid clicking of shoes on the marble floor.

Bellanger said, "Ah, Alessia, thank you for being so prompt."

When the plump woman with short blond hair and large, round glasses finally arrived at the desk, she smiled and said, "Not at all, Garth." Alessia Rossi wore a dark blue pantsuit, and had a tan shirt in her right hand. Speaking with an Italian accent, Rossi turned and said, "Mr. Bryant, it is an honor to meet you. I admire your courage."

Bryant seemed taken off-guard, but replied, "Um, well, thanks, Dr. Rossi."

She continued to smile, and said, "Please call me Alessia."

Bryant nodded, adding, "Yeah, sure, and it's Hunter."

Rossi then said, "Well, Hunter, your shirt."

"What? Oh, right." He smiled and shook his head.

Bryant stood up and began to unbutton the light blue shirt he had now worn since Thursday morning. Bellanger and Rossi watched as the medium-build Bryant finished undoing the last button, slipped it off, and handed the shirt over to Rossi. He said, "That might be a little ripe by now."

Rossi smiled and replied, "I am sure it is fine."

Bryant ran a hand through his thick brown hair, while standing shirtless. Both Rossi and Bellanger had their eyes trained on the shirt that Bryant had removed – the shirt that housed stolen files from the Central Intelligence Agency.

Rossi finally handed the tan shirt over to Bryant.

He said, "Thanks."

Bellanger responded, "No, thank you, Hunter. Thank you for all you have done, and in the face of great danger."

Bryant smiled as he buttoned up the tan shirt.

Bellanger looked at Rossi, "Alessia, you have what you need?"

"I do. Thank you." She turned with the shirt in hand, and began the trek back to the office door.

After Rossi left and Bryant sat back down, a more serious look came across Bellanger's face. "We've discussed this before, Hunter. And I know you understand what this means for you. It will not be easy. You'll become a target. But as I promised before, I will keep you safe, not to mention comfortable."

Bryant said, "I get it. And thanks again, Garth, not just for what you're doing for me, but for exposing the secrets and the lies of the United States."

The grave expression on Bellanger's face gave way to a wide smile. "But make no mistake, I know, and countless others will come to know, that you, my friend, are a true hero of the people."

Bryant's smile broadened, and he sat up straighter in the chair. "We're going to teach those arrogant bastards a few lessons. They're going to pay."

Chapter 6

Since his days as a Navy SEAL and then with the Central Intelligence Agency, Stephen Grant had been a light sleeper. His green eyes opened at any noise out of the ordinary. Fortunately, if reassured that nothing was awry, Grant also could fall back to sleep quickly.

The ability to return to sleep had helped him in the years as a pastor since leaving the Agency. If he received a call from a parishioner, or had to journey to a home or hospital in the middle of the night, barring something nagging at him, Grant could immediately grab some shut eye once back in bed.

As for waking at the slightest noise, that now helped him as a married man. Even with his smartphone on vibrate, Stephen would still wake up to answer a call, while Jennifer's rest remained undisturbed.

That was the case now – early on Monday morning.

Stephen picked up the phone from his nightstand and looked at the screen.

It's 2:25 in the morning, and Sean is calling.

Stephen quietly slipped out of bed, and exited the bedroom.

With Sean, it could be a family matter, a threat to the country, or countless things in between.

Sean McEnany was a unique member of Stephen's congregation at St. Mary's Lutheran Church on the eastern end of Long Island. After the Army Rangers, Sean worked at CorpSecQuest, part legitimate business, part CIA front, and then partnered with Paige Caldwell and Charlie

Driessen in CDM International Strategies and Security. He also headed up the evangelism committee at St. Mary's.

Stephen answered the call. "Sean, what's up? Is everything okay?"

The voice on the other end of the call wasn't Sean.

"Stephen, I'm worried about Sean."

"Rachel, what's happening?"

Before they got married, Rachel also worked the national security game. She decided, though, that with the arrival of children, she would replace the danger of espionage with the challenges of being a preschool teacher and making sure that at least one parent was always home for their children. Recently, however, she also started working with Stephen on a campaign to bring attention to and countering Christian persecution – the Lutheran Response to Christian Persecution.

"Have you heard from Paige or Sean on Hunter Bryant?"

"No. I have no idea what's going on."

Rachel paused, and then said, "Okay, well, I'll leave that up to Sean."

There's a nervousness in her voice.

"Rachel, what's wrong? What do you need me to do?"

"I'm sorry, Stephen. Sean is in a dark place. He's never been like this before – even when Lis died." Lis Dicce was killed while working for CDM. "And for the first time, I can't seem to reach him. Can you come over and talk to him?"

"I'll be right over."

"Thanks."

As he put on jeans, slipped a polo shirt over his fit body, and ran a comb through his black hair, Stephen woke Jennifer up. He told her what little he knew. She followed him to the front door, kissed him, and said, "I'll say a prayer for Sean."

It took less than 10 minutes for Stephen to arrive at the McEnany home. Given Sean's work, the house ranked as the most secure on Long Island – though no one would know that from the outside, or for that matter, if they were inside.

As he approached, Rachel opened the front door. "Thank you, again, for coming."

"I'm here for you guys."

They exchanged a brief hug, and Rachel said, "He's in the basement, not in his office but at the bar. He's been down there for hours – more than seven hours, actually – and won't come up. And beyond the basics of what happened, he won't talk to me."

Wow. That's not Sean.

Grant thought he would try to get more on what had occurred. "And why?"

She stared at her pastor and friend briefly, and then said, "He's going to tell you."

It's hard to shake the need-to-know that's hammered into those of us who worked in intelligence – which, of course, shows the training we received.

Rachel added, "But you do need to know..."

Grant could see that she was working to hold back tears. She continued barely above a whisper. "He's lost people."

Oh, dear Lord.

Grant simply replied, "Okay. I understand." He patted her arm, and turned to the stairs.

He had descended these stairs before in the McEnany home. Sometimes, Grant was visiting to enjoy a few hours of relaxation with friends in the main part of the basement, which featured a poker table, large screen television with an assortment of comfortable chairs, a billiards table, and a bar. It all had a vague Vegas feel to it. At other times, Grant would move by all of that and enter a utility closet. That small room housed a metal door, with a key pad, touch screen and video security system. When that system allowed entry, it meant passing into one of the most secure home offices on the planet, including state-of-the-art computer and telecommunications equipment, along with a mini-arsenal.

When Grant reached the bottom of the stairs, he saw Sean sitting in one of the chairs pointed at the large screen.

However, the television was off. In fact, only one light was on – a standing lamp next to Sean's chair.

Stephen started to move toward the chair, which was facing in the opposite direction.

Sean didn't turn around. He merely said, "Stephen. So, Rachel called you to come over and talk to me."

Stephen stopped a few feet to Sean's left. "Something like that. How are you?"

Sean didn't answer. Instead, he took a big gulp out of the glass in his right hand.

Scotch?

Never a man of many words, Sean said in his raspy voice, "You're here. Grab a seat."

"Thanks." Stephen sat in the chair next to Sean's.

Sean proceeded to drain the last bit of Scotch from the glass. He stood up and started toward the bar. Stephen noted a distinct swaying.

Sean asked, "Want a drink?"

"A small one."

Sean never inquired as to what Stephen preferred. Rather, he just poured another glass of Scotch, in addition to his own refill. He came back, handed Stephen the glass, and sat back down.

Stephen said, "Thanks."

Sean merely raised his glass in response, and then took a gulp of the liquid.

After taking a sip of his drink, Stephen asked, "So, what happened?"

"You don't know?"

Grant shook his head, and replied, "No."

"Well, it'll be all over the news soon enough."

Stephen waited.

After taking another long drink from his glass, Sean said, "A fucking traitor at the CIA."

Stephen's mindset shifted back to his Agency days. "Details."

Sean looked over at Stephen. "Yeah, okay. Well, this little shit, Hunter Bryant, apparently downloaded a list of the people the CIA works with, our 'assets,' if you like that word, around the Pacific Rim, including China and North Korea. And he walked out the front door with it."

Stephen whispered, "Crap."

Sean took another gulp of Scotch. "So, this little asshole emailed that he wasn't coming into work on Friday. His supervisor is pissed because that breaks policy. Thankfully, she starts poking around, and they find out what this guy did. But by that point, he's out of the country, and we find out that he's working with Garth Bellanger."

Stephen interjected, "The 'Free Garth' idiot who steals information and spreads it across the Internet and calls it 'free speech'?"

"The same. But Bellanger's even sleazier than his already-sleazy reputation. After stealing information, he then picks and chooses what goes public, and what he can privately sell to boost his already fat bank account."

Stephen's mind wandered back to Sean's state for a moment. *He's apparently been drinking for hours, but his mind is still pretty clear. And he talks more now than when sober.* He shook his attention back to Bryant and Bellanger. "I heard that about him."

"Yeah, so much for 'Free Garth' liberating information, being a champion of transparency and the rest of that shit." Sean drained his glass, once more, and said, "I'm getting another."

There's no way he's been drinking at this pace for hours.

Stephen stood up and went to take the glass from his friend. "Stay there. I'll get it."

Sean protested, "I can get it for myself."

Ah, there's a bit of the drunk.

Stephen replied, "I know, but I'll pour you another while you tell me more. What's been the fallout?"

Sean gave up his glass. "Fallout? Shit." He stared blankly for several seconds, and then his face flashed anger. "Already people have died – murdered by the Chinese government."

Stephen handed over a glass containing half of the Scotch than what Sean had previously poured himself. "I'm sorry."

"Yeah." Sean closed his eyes and sat back in the chair. He remained quiet for nearly a minute. And then without opening his eyes, he spoke, "They murdered Ping Ho, a journalist, and his wife and three children." He went quiet again.

Dear Lord.

Sean eventually spoke barely above a whisper. "Ping truly loved China, and wanted to see it free one day, you know, for his children. He actually was the one who warned me about the MSS getting ready to arrest Andy Faan in Hong Kong last month. Ping was the reason why Faan wasn't taken away, and either murdered, or tortured and put in a dark cell not to be heard from again."

"Sean, I'm so sorry."

Sean looked at Stephen. The anger was unmistakable. He said, "You know what's worse, Stephen? He wasn't one of the first people I contacted when I got word from the Agency about what had happened. He was close to the top, but not at the very top of the list. I tried to prioritize it in a way that I thought made sense."

"Of course."

"Well, I was on the phone with Ping telling him what had happened. I just finished relaying what Bryant had done, including who he handed the information over to, when Ping said that government vehicles were pulling up in front of his home." Sean's hands began to shake as he tried to take another drink. He stopped, looked down at the glass, and then jumped to his feet and hurled the glass at the television on the wall. The glass shattered and the screen cracked with pieces falling off. Sean struggled for a moment to maintain his balance, and then he turned and looked down at Stephen. "I was on the phone with him! I told him to get out, to get his family out. But it was too late. He knew it, and I knew it. His voice shook, but he actually thanked me for what I had done for him and his country. Then he said if there was anything that I could do to help his family to get out of the country, he would appreciate it. He didn't wait for an answer. Ping said, 'I pray that my wife and children will survive.' The call ended before I could apologize, before I could tell him that I would try."

Stephen rose out of the chair, and stood just a couple of feet from Sean, looking into a face now drenched in sadness. And then Stephen saw something that he never expected. Tears flowed from the eyes of Sean McEnany.

Sean said, "I would have gotten his family out."

"I know you would have, Sean."

"But I couldn't. I got word just a couple of hours later that Ping and his entire family were executed – even the kids."

He fell forward into the arms of his friend and pastor. Stephen held him up while Sean wept.

Stephen prayed silently for his friend, for Rachel and their children, and for everyone else hurt by Hunter Bryant and Garth Bellanger.

After talking a bit more with Sean, and then helping Rachel get him into bed, Grant was alone, driving back home in his Jeep Wrangler.

Assorted thoughts ran through his mind – some from Pastor Stephen Grant and others from Grant the former SEAL and CIA operative. He parked the Jeep on the circular driveway between the house and a three-car garage, and sat still for a few moments.

And what happens when Sean gets clear of the sadness, or more accurately, what does he use the sadness and anger for? You know, Grant, what he's going to do, not to mention that Paige and Charlie will be at his side.

Chapter 7

When he entered the house, it was just after 6:00 AM. Jennifer was drinking tea with her laptop open, sitting at the kitchen island. She rose from her chair, kissed Stephen on the cheek, and asked, "How is Sean?"

"To be honest, I've never seen him like this. In fact, before this, I never could have imagined him being in such a state." He went on to tell Jennifer all that had happened.

After listening to her husband, she could only manage saying, "Dear God, that's terrible."

Stephen nodded. He went to the refrigerator, removed a pitcher, and poured himself an iced tea.

Jennifer asked, "Do you want me to make something for breakfast?"

"No, thanks. Besides, you've got a call with one of President Orlov's economic policy people shortly, right?" Stephen and Jennifer had come to know Russian President Vitaly Orlov during and after a deadly struggle for control of the country. Orlov appreciated Jennifer's book, and she had done some teaching in Russia – both students at Moscow State University and some of Orlov's policy people.

"Yes. It's scheduled for an hour from now."

"Go to work. I'm going to call Paige to see what more I can learn, and pass on what kind of state Sean is in, if they aren't aware. And then I'm supposed to meet the guys at the diner."

"Okay. Let me know if you need anything." Jennifer went down the hall to her office, while Stephen pulled out his encrypted phone and called Paige Caldwell.

Paige answered, "Stephen. You spoke to Sean."

"Yes. I just left him. He's not in a good place. I've certainly never seen him this way, but more importantly, Rachel hasn't either."

"I know. I spoke to her while you were with Sean. I'm sitting in the office with Charlie, so I'm putting you on speaker." The CDM offices covered the top floor of an office building in Crystal City, Virginia, across the Potomac from Washington, D.C., and across I-395 from the Pentagon.

"Alright," responded Stephen.

Other than Jennifer and the small circle of clergy friends he was scheduled to have breakfast with shortly, Paige and Charlie were the two people he knew best in life and could count on for nearly anything. He had worked with each of them during his Agency days, as well as on certain occasions in recent years. Long before he met Jennifer, Stephen and Paige not only were official partners at the CIA, but they also were in the bedroom. Since she came back into his life, Paige and Stephen had moved to a close friendship, with Jennifer also calling Paige a friend. At times, for Stephen, it became a little awkward, while both Jennifer and Paige seemed to relish the fact that it made him feel that way.

Once the call moved onto the speaker, Charlie Driessen said, "Grant, just how screwed up is Sean?"

Stephen was well aware that Charlie had a certain way of putting things. "He's taking it hard." Stephen went on to provide the details that Paige and Charlie needed as Sean's friends and colleagues, without revealing anything that Sean wouldn't want told.

Charlie then commented, "When he sobers up, he'll be looking for blood."

Paige added, "Damn right. I'm with him."

Driessen grunted his approval, while Grant agreed in his head but restrained himself from saying anything.

Stephen asked, "What about Zhu Gao's people?"

From a base of operations in Santa Cruz, California, Gao had run a small network of people inside and outside China who were ready to act against the communist regime. After

Gao died in a confrontation with Chinese spies just a short time ago, CDM took over his operation.

Paige answered, "Thankfully, they're all still good. Gao never handed his contacts over to the Agency, and neither have we. It drove Tank nuts, but it wound up saving lives this time." Tank Hoard, whom all three had worked with at the Agency, remained in the CIA, and had climbed many rungs on the ladder. He served as the CIA's primary contact for CDM.

Stephen said, "Thank God. But speaking of lives, do we know how many were lost, in addition to Ping Ho and his family?"

There was a moment of silence before Paige replied. "The rest of Sean's contacts, according to Sean, are okay. He said that he never gave their names to the Agency, and was bitter for having told Tank about Ping."

Charlie added, "I had three people in China; one with a family. I hammered away that they needed quick escape plans in case something like this happened. They listened and they're out. I told Hoard that he better make sure they get set up okay."

Stephen commented, "Tank has to feel awful."

Paige said, "He will. They don't have time for that right now. And when Bellanger goes public with some of this stuff, they're going to get all kinds of shit. But getting back to your question, Tank said that there are roughly a half-dozen assets they've lost contact with in China. But it could get worse, given that some of the operations were set up for less frequent contact."

Lord, please be with them.

Stephen asked, "What about North Korea?"

Paige said, "Yeah, that's the mystery at this point. We know that Bellanger works with the Chinese, but no one is really sure about his contacts with North Korea."

Charlie chimed in, "That's hopeful bullshit. If the Chinese know, they're going to make sure the North Koreans know."

Stephen knew that Charlie was right.

Paige said, "Tank didn't have any hard information yet. That's where our people are going to suffer the most."

"What about other countries around the Pacific?" asked Stephen.

Paige said, "Tank expects that will be the stuff that Bellanger will dump publicly. The U.S. is on good terms with most of those nations, but we still have our assets. So, that'll serve Bellanger's public persona as exposing supposedly nefarious doings – thanks to Hunter Bryant."

"That's still going to be a mess," interjected Charlie.

"President Links has been working the phones with our allies to give them a heads up on what's happened," added Paige.

President Adam Links had worked years ago at the CIA, after Stephen had moved on from the Agency. While at the CIA, Links and Paige had struck up a clandestine relationship. And after years of cooling off, that affair resumed more recently, to the point that the two were now secretly engaged, with very few people, including Stephen and the CDM group, knowing.

Charlie said, "Well, glad to see your boyfriend is making a contribution." Charlie enjoyed tweaking Paige about her relationship with the president.

Paige ignored Charlie's comment, as she usually did, and then said, "Alright, well, Stephen, if you can keep an eye on Sean, that would be great. We're still trying to help limit the damage. Once we get beyond the emergency stage of this mess, Chase is going to head up to Long Island to work with Sean." Chase Axelrod had been brought into CDM by McEnany.

"Okay. Let me know if there's something else I can do."

Paige replied, "I guess you're covering the prayer and counseling end of things." She ended the call.

Stephen showered and then drove to the diner where he regularly gathered with his three friends for morning devotions and breakfast. He tried not to be distracted by the fact that he couldn't tell, at least not yet, Father Tom Stone,

Father Ron McDermott, and Pastor Zack Charmichael anything that was happening.

However, among the devotional readings from *For All the Saints: A Prayer Book For and By the Church* that the four covered was Psalm 7. Stephen wound up pondering part of that psalm for the rest of the day:

> *God is my shield and defense,*
> *he is the savior of the true in heart.*
> *God is a righteous judge;*
> *God sits in judgment every day.*
> *If they will not repent, God will whet his sword;*
> *he will bend his bow and make it ready.*
> *He has prepared his weapons of death;*
> *he makes his arrows shafts of fire.*
> *Look at those who are in labor with wickedness,*
> *who conceive evil, and give birth to a lie.*
> *They dig a pit and make it deep*
> *and fall into the hole that they have made.*
> *Their malice turns back upon their own head;*
> *their violence falls on their own scalp.*
> *I will bear witness that the Lord is righteous;*
> *I will praise the name of the Lord Most High.*

Chapter 8

Members of the international media filled the ornate banquet room on the ground floor of an exclusive Paris hotel. They came to hear from the two men sitting at a table on a raised stage.

Garth Bellanger and Hunter Bryant made for an unusual pair. The bald Bellanger was dressed, as usual, in sneakers, jeans and forest green t-shirt, and clearly relished the attention. Meanwhile, the youthful self confidence that Hunter Bryant had exhibited since arriving at Bellanger's estate evaporated when stepping onto the stage and being hit with lights and shouted questions. He looked distinctly uncomfortable.

*   *   *

The president of North Korea – who, of course, was a communist dictator with an iron grip on all aspects of life in the country – sat at an enormous desk in a high-ceilinged office. This particular palace was located outside Pyongyang, and was surrounded by sprawling acreage that separated the building from the crippling poverty of his country.

The president had received a list of 17 names from the Chinese the prior day.

A dozen of the people on the list had been tracked down already, and terminated per his orders. Three individuals could not be found, which infuriated the president. But his greatest rage was being saved for two others who actually served on his personal staff.

The two awaited their fates. One of those was Sang-jun Park.

*   *   *

Bellanger had much of the media wrapped around his finger, speaking with a smooth confidence. "Make no mistake, my friends, Hunter Bryant is a hero. He is a hero for all of us who love and treasure freedom and transparency. He is a hero to those of us who oppose the global elitists, technological monopolists, and capitalist dictators."

*   *   *

Park's hands were bound, and he was being pushed into the president's office.

The short, fat dictator rose from his chair, and picked up a 16th-century jedok geom sword with a single-edge, four-foot blade. He then came around his desk, and kind of waddled toward a chair in the middle of the room.

Park had a look of fear on his face coming into the office. He was being prodded along by four military guards. But while looking at the president, Park's expression gave way to resignation. He took a deep breath, and then started walking toward his fate without being nudged.

*   *   *

Bellanger finished a rhetorical attack on the United States, and then turned to Bryant, and said, "Hunter, I'm sure you have a few things to say." Bellanger smiled broadly.

Bryant moved around in his chair, and was sweating. He started to reply, "Yes..." But then he stopped to clear his throat. He reached for the crystal glass filled with iced mineral water on the table in front of him. His hand shook ever so slightly as he raised the glass and took a drink.

After putting the water down, Bryant said, "Yes, thank you, Garth. I know people are going to accuse me of terrible things. But none of them are true. I am not a traitor, as many will claim, but instead, I am the true patriot."

It was clear that Bryant started shaking off the nerves, and was becoming more comfortable.

He continued, "I am ashamed to say that I worked at the Central Intelligence Agency. I did so thinking that I would be helping to protect the American people from threats around the world. However, I eventually learned that the real threat was the United States government against the world, and against the American people. The U.S. government treats the world like its sandbox where it can go play a deadly game with innocent lives. That's evident from the list of names that I secured and Garth released here today. I mean, why is the U.S. spying on its supposed allies? It's insane. Americans wonder why their country has so many enemies. It's because the U.S. government rampages around the world, telling others what to do, imposing, or trying to impose, its will on others. The U.S. government is the greatest tyrannical entity in the world today. I had to do something about this. I was in a position to make a difference, and had a moral imperative to act."

*   *   *

The president said, "Sit down, Mr. Park."

Park sat in the chair.

The president nodded at the guards, and two stepped forward to bind Park to the chair. When finished, Park's hands, arms and legs were fully constrained, only his head moved freely.

The president looked at Park, and declared, "You are guilty of betraying your leader. And since I am this nation, you are guilty of betraying everyone in our country."

Park stared straight ahead, and didn't respond.

The president's anger grew. "I am this country. I am your god. What gave you the right to turn on me?"

Park finally spoke. "You are insane. Your father was insane, and so was your grandfather. I tried to act to free our people from your madness, from your..."

The president leaned in close to Park's face, and screamed, "Shut up! How dare you!"

Park went quiet, once more.

The president said, "I have perfected my skills with the jedok geom. And now you will suffer my justice, with your head being separated from your body."

Park closed his eyes.

*　　*　　*

A reporter raised his hand, and Bellanger pointed to him, and said, "Yes, your question?"

The reporter stood up and asked, "Mr. Bryant, about your father being a retired U.S. Army officer, your brother in the Navy, and your sister, I believe, works for the FBI – are they part of the problem then? You know, guilty of everything that you accuse the U.S. of being?"

"Um, excuse me?"

"You come from a family steeped in the military and law enforcement, so aren't they part of the problem?"

Bryant hesitated, but finally said, "Well, members of my family are not policymakers."

The reporter pressed, "So, the fact that they choose to carry out the policies, that's alright?"

"Well..."

Bellanger stepped in. "The point at 'Free Garth' has always been about the decisionmakers."

The reporter persisted, "Based on Mr. Bryant's actions, though, it would seem that he is saying that everyone that is a part of the system has a decision to make."

Bellanger replied, "Well, yes, but not everyone can be as courageous as Hunter Bryant. You must understand that

Hunter will be relentlessly pursued by these powerful forces."

*   *   *

The president screamed in fury, and swung the sword. But his claims of great skill did not materialize, which was unfortunate for Sang-jun Park, as his suffering was prolonged.

The turned blade hacked into Park's neck. He screamed in pain.

The president's rage intensified, which was evident through his subsequent horrific actions. He continued to swing the sword at Park's neck. He cut away at skin, flesh and bone. On the fourth impact, death arrived for Park. On the fifth, his body fell over. Each guard took a couple of steps back, and one averted his eyes. The dictator of North Korea continued hacking away until the blade happened to be properly positioned, cutting through what remained of nerve and bone, with Park's head finally separating from his body and rolling several inches away.

Chapter 9

On a Sunday night two weeks after Garth Bellanger provided the Chinese with part of the information stolen by Hunter Bryant, and released the rest of the classified material to the world, Stephen Grant found himself feeling agitated during a moment meant for some relaxation. Over the previous fortnight, it seemed like this had become his default mood.

Stephen was sitting next to Jennifer on their living room couch watching a baseball playoff game. Jennifer was fully engrossed, given that her team, the Cardinals, were playing. Stephen, however, was going over in his mind what was happening with Sean McEnany.

I haven't heard from him since that night he was drunk, reacting to the murders of Ping Ho and his family. He hasn't been at church; not returning my calls. Rachel says he's totally immersed in tracking down Hunter Bryant, and has been on the road. Although, I'm not sure if she's holding off telling me things, or if Sean is holding off telling Rachel.

Jennifer interrupted his reflections. "I know this isn't the Reds, but you're usually engaged in the game, even if it's rooting against my Cardinals. What are you thinking about?"

Stephen breathed in deeply. "I'm sorry."

"You're thinking about Sean?"

Stephen nodded. "But I'm a multi-tasker, and noting that your Cardinals look flat. As a Reds fan, I'm kind of torn between enjoying this fact, and feeling bad for you."

Jennifer leaned her head on his shoulder, patted his chest, and said, "You're such a caring husband, I guess."

They both smiled, and continued watching the game.

I get where Sean is right now, and what he's doing. Heck, there's a significant part of me that wants to be next to him, helping to track down and capture Hunter Bryant, not to mention Garth Bellanger. While the media has stopped caring about the situation, the fallout continues. I wonder what the latest is. I should call Paige.

Stephen said, "Jen, I'm going to take a minute and..."

She interrupted, "... call Paige to find out the latest." She looked up and smiled at him.

He kissed her on the forehead, got up from the couch, and went into the kitchen.

Paige answered the call saying, "Stephen, it's Sunday night. Shouldn't you be exhausted from your church stuff and spending time with your wife? Why are you calling your old CIA lover?"

She's in full "Paige" mode, apparently.

Stephen responded, "Right, and am I intruding on time with your fiancé?"

"This was more fun when I could make you uncomfortable and you didn't have something on me. What's up?"

"I was just thinking about Sean."

"Yeah, well, you're not alone there. He's in dark and deep."

"What does that mean?"

"Sean is obsessed with getting Bryant and Bellanger, and while Charlie and I are right there with him, his obsession has taken on a quality that even troubles me."

"And that's saying something."

"I'll ignore that. Anyway, Chase is with him each step of the way, and is keeping the rest of us up to date. But if he wasn't there, Sean would be on a lone-man crusade, I think. Chase is trying to keep him grounded."

"You're not making me feel any better."

Paige replied, "Well, it is what it is. What about you? Have you talked with Sean at all? After all, you're his pastor."

"Thanks. No, he hasn't returned any of my calls. Rachel only tells me that he's tracking down Bryant and traveling."

"That's an understatement. But I don't think he's telling her much, either."

None of this is good.

Stephen shifted direction slightly. "What's the latest read on the damage Bryant has done?"

"A few people we were working with managed to escape North Korea – an incredible feat, quite frankly. And some got out of China as well. But the tally of those dead or unlikely to ever see the light of day again is estimated at 14 in North Korea, and 22 in China, and that's probably a conservative estimate."

"Dear God."

"There are diplomatic challenges that Adam has to deal with among other countries as well. But the hands of both Bryant and Bellanger are covered in blood. They have a lot to answer for; and they need to answer for it."

"I agree. So, what are the problems we're facing in making that happen?"

"We're facing" – really, Grant?

Paige said, "First, the French aren't cooperating. They like Bellanger and his business. Second, according to Chase, Sean doesn't have people who are inside or have close contact with Bellanger's operation. And that leads into the third challenge. We do know that Bellanger isn't taking any chances with Bryant's safety, and he's got a team protecting and moving him around constantly. But as to where, it remains a mystery. The CIA and Sean are getting some assistance from various intelligence services in Europe, but it's limited and being done very quietly. Many Europeans buy into Bellanger's spiel, including his line that Bryant is some kind of hero. So, politicians across Europe are either praising Bellanger, or just keeping quiet on the entire matter. They certainly aren't looking to have people in their governments being exposed as supporting CIA efforts to get Garth Bellanger or Hunter Bryant."

"It's amazing that European politicians can often make American politicians look good."

"It's all relative."

"Well, in the case of politicians, I'll agree with you." He couldn't resist, adding, "What does President Links think about your views on such matters?"

"You're funny, but he gets it."

"And what's going on with Bryant's family? I saw that a statement was released. It had to be hard to admit being horrified by traitorous actions by a son and brother."

"Adam spoke to Bryant's father, Vincent, the retired colonel."

Even though I know President Links and am one of the few people who know their story, it's still kind of weird to hear Paige refer to him as "Adam."

Paige continued, "He said the colonel was sad, disappointed and apologetic, that his wife was bewildered and worried, and that his two other children were deeply angered by their brother." She sighed. "You're right, of course, it's always hard on the family and friends when someone turns against their country, but in a family like this, it has to be mind-blowing."

Grant agreed, but he also had seen upheaval and shock delivered to many individuals over the years by family and close friends. Stephen asked Paige to keep him in the loop if anything changed regarding Sean, and they ended the call.

When Stephen returned to the couch, the Cardinals had the bases loaded, and were down by two runs. Jen asked, "What did she say?"

Stephen smiled ever so slightly, and answered, "Unfortunately, nothing too surprising. I'll give you the rundown after we see how this bases loaded situation comes out."

Chapter 10

Sean McEnany and Chase Axelrod pulled up in a black Mercedes-Benz G-Class SUV. Axelrod parked the vehicle on the narrow street in a manufacturing town in the most eastern region of Germany.

As the two men got out, McEnany said, "I'll take the lead on this."

Axelrod replied, "I know I'm the tall black guy and you're the blond-haired one, but if he doesn't speak English, I'm guessing then I'll have to take the lead. That is, unless you've been secretly learning German."

McEnany simply replied, "Fine." He knocked on the front door of one of the small rowhouses.

A heavy, balding man in his early fifties opened the door, and appeared unphased by the two men standing in front of him. He said, in German, "Yes. Can I help you?"

Axelrod began, "Thank you. Yes, I hope you can. We..."

McEnany interrupted, "English. Do you speak English?"

The man didn't respond immediately. He took a closer look at McEnany and Axelrod, as well as glancing up and down the street. "Yes, I do."

McEnany continued, "We're in need of accommodations, and we've been told that you're a man who can supply what we need for the right price." McEnany took a half-step forward, and moved his head to also look up and down the street. "Can we come in to discuss this? As you can imagine, we're here because we are in need of confidentiality."

The overweight German stepped to the side, and said, "Come in."

After McEnany and Axelrod were inside, the German closed the door. He asked, "How did you wind up coming to me?"

McEnany replied, "What do you mean?"

The German sighed in some exasperation. "Who sent you?"

McEnany said, "Garth Bellanger."

After only the slightest of hesitations, the German donned a quizzical expression. He said, "I don't know who that is. I'm sorry, you will have to leave."

McEnany responded, "Oh, I'm sorry to hear you say that." He quickly reached inside his jacket, and pulled out a Glock. He grabbed the German by the arm, and shoved the barrel of the gun into one of the man's chins. McEnany whispered, "Keep your mouth shut." He then nodded at Axelrod, who also had his gun drawn.

While McEnany guided the German into the kitchen, Axelrod proceeded to check the rest of the house.

By the time Axelrod entered the kitchen, McEnany had already bound the German's hands. Chase reported, "The house is clear."

McEnany merely nodded in response, and then turned to the German. "Well, Mr. Franz Schneider, you've done an able job at keeping the services you provide quiet. We had to do a great deal of investigation, but someone always gives you up."

Schneider replied, "I have no idea what you are talking about, and you will pay a heavy price for this invasion."

McEnany said, "Yes, I'm sure we will. But in the meantime, I need information from you. Let's start with Hunter Bryant."

"Who?" asked Schneider.

"About two weeks ago, you provided accommodations to Hunter Bryant, the former CIA officer who stole information from the United States."

Schneider smiled. "Ah, now that I think about it, I have heard of this Bryant. You have the wrong information about me. I have never met the man, but I do admire him."

"Hmmm. You admire traitors who get people murdered?"

"From what I have heard, he merely exposed what the American government did not want made public. You know, the American government again doing things it should not, preying on the weak and abusing its power to get what it wants."

Axelrod interjected, "That's kind of ironic coming from a German, you know, given your history."

Schneider shrugged his shoulders. "Governments are the same everywhere."

Axelrod persisted, "So, the German government of today is the same as the Nazis? And the U.S. government is the same, for example, as the regimes in North Korea and China?"

"For the most part, yes, that is the case," answered Schneider. "You Americans like to point out the atrocities committed by the North Koreans and Chinese, but you are no different. You have your own atrocities."

McEnany said, "So, there's no difference between the U.S. and North Korea?"

"In the end, no, there is not."

McEnany looked at Axelrod and said, "So, we're dealing with a 'Free Garth' true believer here. What an idiot."

Schneider immediately shifted from calm to anger. "Mr. Bellanger is doing the right thing. He is a voice for the powerless against the tyranny of capitalists and those they control in government."

"You admire this Garth Bellanger?"

"Of course, I do."

"That's ridiculous. Why would you even be part of his network?"

"I am proud to be part of what he is working for."

McEnany looked at Axelrod, and then back to Schneider. "Well, Franz, thanks for confirming that you're working with Bellanger. We're going to need to know everything. Who is your contact with Bellanger? Where did you set Bryant up? Who was with Bryant? And so on."

Schneider spat back, "Go to hell!"

McEnany pointed his gun at Schneider's knee. "You're going to give me the information I want, Franz."

Axelrod stood up a little straighter and cleared his throat. Schneider's expression changed. The anger disappeared, with a trace of fear emerging. "Go ahead." His voice shook ever so slightly. "Prove that I am correct; that you Americans are no better than the North Koreans or the Chinese."

"Franz. You really aren't all that bright, are you? You see, I'm working outside the American system. I am an individual who has gone rogue. I am seeking revenge, and I'll do just about anything to get what I want. That, of course, should worry you, Franz. But just to finish our little chat on this topic, the difference is that what I might have to do to you would not be approved by the U.S. government, nor your German government. In contrast, the entire systems in places like North Korea and China are built on this kind of abuse of power, use of fear, and, yes, murder. Do you get the difference, Franz?"

Axelrod took a step forward, and said, "Sean?"

"Shut up, Chase. I'm in the midst of teaching Franz a lesson."

Axelrod's face was a mix of worry and questions.

McEnany moved his face closer to Schneider's. He said, "You see what's going on here, Franz? Chase doesn't like where I'm headed. He is still a civilized man. There are lines he will not cross. Now, don't underestimate him. I've seen this guy in action, and he's a badass. But unlike that little shit of a dictator in North Korea and the government in China, and right now, me, he is restrained by right and wrong."

Axelrod's stare now remained on McEnany, rather than on Schneider. Chase also gripped his weapon a bit more tightly.

McEnany continued, "At the same time, Chase isn't all that sure if what I'm saying is true or not. Just like you're wondering right now. So, he's not going to stop me before I pull this trigger and obliterate your knee, or..." McEnany shifted the gun, now pushing it against Schneider's genitals. "Or, perhaps shooting something that even a fat, fifty-something such as yourself still thinks is valuable."

Schneider's breathing grew more labored.

"So, what's it going to be, Franz?"

After Franz Schneider answered all of McEnany's questions, Axelrod tied up the German's legs and arms, and made sure his hands remained secure. At the same time, McEnany called a contact in the German Federal Intelligence Service to let him know that Franz Schneider was now available for pick up.

After getting back in the Mercedes SUV, the two men drove in silence for a few minutes. Axelrod finally asked, "What the hell was that back there?"

"I was acquiring information we needed."

"And was all that shit you fed Schneider true or not?"

McEnany didn't answer.

After a few minutes, Axelrod asked, "Well?"

McEnany responded, "Just drive."

Chapter 11

When one of the smartphones on her desk began to rumble, Paige Caldwell looked at the name on the screen. She answered, "Stephen, how are you?"

"I'm doing okay. You?" replied Stephen Grant.

"Juggling a few challenges, including Sean."

"That's actually why I was calling. I'm heading out on a trip late tonight, and will be away for about three weeks. I wanted to talk with Sean before I left, but he's still not getting back to me."

"Well, I don't think you're alone on that front. He seems to be only speaking with people who have something that can help in tracking down Hunter Bryant."

"I still can't believe that Bryant hasn't been found yet."

Caldwell replied, "It's been less than a month. Do I have to remind you how long it took to get bin Laden?"

"I get it. Is Sean's head in a somewhat better place, at least?"

Caldwell sighed, and said, "I was beginning to think so, but then Chase passed on some disturbing facts about how Sean chose to interrogate someone working with Bellanger."

Not good.

"Speaking of Bellanger, it's no secret where he is. What's stopping Sean from getting to him?"

"At this point, basic common sense. He'd like to do a hell of a lot more than just bring Bellanger to the U.S. for prosecution. But he knows that it wouldn't end well if he tried to get to Bellanger. I reminded him of this fact, and his response was along the lines of 'I know that, Paige. I'm not an idiot.'"

"I have the feeling that his restraint on Bellanger has more to do with making sure he gets Bryant first."

"That's likely part of it. But Sean, for all of his anger right now, has no death wish. He's not so far gone that he wants to leave Rachel without a husband, and their kids without a father."

"Thank God for that much."

Caldwell didn't respond.

Grant was quiet for a moment as well, and then asked, "When you talk to Sean, can you let him know that we spoke and that I'd like to talk with him?"

"Sure, I'll do that tonight."

"Thanks. That's appreciated."

"Where are you headed on the trip?"

"I'm going on a retreat to a monastery in France."

Caldwell laughed, and said, "You're heading to Europe, and that's where I'm trying to bring Sean back from after his unusual interrogation technique yesterday. Maybe you can take over for him."

"I don't think I'll find Hunter Bryant at the Monastere de Saint Paul."

"Wait. Aren't those the monks with that delicious chocolate?"

Really? Does everyone know about this chocolate?

"That's what I've been told."

"Did you know that they're not on the Internet, and have very limited distribution in the U.S.?"

"I was somewhat aware."

"Do you think Jennifer would mind if you brought some chocolates back for your ex-CIA lover?"

Grant sighed. "Paige, haven't we moved beyond this?"

"I certainly have, but I'm not sure about you ... lover."

"Paige, I have five words for you."

"Ooooh. What are they?"

"President Adam Links, your fiancé."

"You're no fun."

"Yeah, and thank God I'm not." He paused, and added, "And yes, I can bring back chocolates for you."

Grant knew that Caldwell was enjoying this, and smiling brightly.

"Thanks, Stephen. We'll talk soon. And if Bryant turns up at the monastery, I'm sure Sean will take your call."

"Goodbye, Paige."

Apparently, I'll be shipping home a good deal of chocolate from France.

Chapter 12

After leaving the autoroute, the drive to the Monastere de Saint Paul proceeded along a narrow two-lane road that rose gradually at first, and then took on a steeper ascent. Stephen Grant was behind the wheel of a four-door Renault Scenic – a rental picked up at Charles de Gaulle Airport. Next to him in the front passenger seat was Father Ron McDermott.

The two men were relatively quiet. Stephen thought about an earlier time he was in France. On the surface, this trip wasn't all that different from that one years ago. There was the drive across the bucolic French countryside. There was relatively little chatter between driver and passenger. And in each case, Stephen was heading to a church for an assignment.

That's certainly where the similarities end.

That CIA assignment had him meeting, and dealing with, a Russian double agent in a small, empty – or nearly empty – church.

Quite a difference from journeying to a monastery for a retreat. But if I hadn't taken that assignment for the Agency would I be here right now? Sometimes I wonder.

After dealing with a Russian general, it was during his return to the United States that Grant first started to give serious thought to making a career change – from the CIA to the Church.

Ron interrupted his reflections. "We're getting close. This is where things get interesting."

The road turned sharply to the left, and Grant found himself on a plateau on the side of the mountain. He looked around at small fields populated by sheep, a few houses and barns, and then the road led into a tiny village. Grant thought that the mix of stone and Tudor-style buildings, the street turning to old stone, the mountain looming large above all of it, and a bridge over a rushing stream made it seem that the place had been transplanted from a fairy tale.

Ron reported, "This is the Village de Saint Paul. The monks actually have a small store here where they sell their famous chocolate."

"I hope they ship their goods across the Atlantic?"

"There's the store." Ron pointed to a small building with a white front, paned window and a dark wood door that matched the roof tiles in color. "Unless they've upgraded since I was here last, the monks don't ship overseas from the store or the monastery."

"Really? How do they distribute this reportedly delicious chocolate?"

Ron shrugged, "They have the store, and the monks' delivery trucks – I think they have three – that they drive down the mountain a couple of times a week, and make deliveries. It really has been a word-of-mouth thing."

Stephen commented, "Well, word-of-mouth has proven pretty successful for these monks. So, I'm taking the chocolate to Fedex or some other delivery service?"

I have met the most interesting monks in recent years – barbequing monks, high-tech monks, wine-producing monks, and now, chocolate-making monks.

Ron nodded, and then said, "As we move beyond the village, the road gets steeper and narrower, with even sharper turns."

Stephen refocused on the surroundings, and said, "This is a beautiful place."

"Just wait until you see what's ahead."

Stephen had to give the Renault extra gas to get up the road. After a horseshoe turn, the car emerged from a thick patch of trees. Stephen wasn't really prepared for what he saw next.

To his right was a field where cows were grazing, and beyond it was a stunning view down onto the countryside they had just driven across. A fence served as a barrier against any cows mistakenly wandering over the side.

On the left was a stone cliffside of the mountain. It rose some 600 feet into the sky. A waterfall streamed down the side of the cliff, with the water collecting in a pond carved out of mountain stone. The water then found its way into a stream that went under another stone bridge, across the field of cows, and then down another, smaller falls to the stream and village below.

On the opposite side of the falls and pond stood the Monastere de Saint Paul.

As Stephen slowly drove the Renault across the little bridge, Ron asked, "What do you think?"

"Spectacular."

"Told you."

A large stone church came out from the side of the mountain, with two towers at the opposite end from the cliff. The monastery church loomed large over a small complex of buildings on the north side, versus the waterfall and pond on the south side. As Stephen looked closer, he saw that the sand-colored stone church didn't simply butt up against the mountain, but was built into the gray rock of the cliff. He wondered how much of this 11th century monastery actually was inside the mountain. "Beautiful and fascinating."

Ron replied, "And more. Wait until you get a closer look and go inside."

Ron directed Stephen to park the car in a small, gravel-covered spot just off the right side of the road. Stephen was more than happy to do so in order to get out and drink in his surroundings.

There was an October nip in the air on this bright, sunny afternoon. After getting out of the car, Grant stretched a bit and breathed in deeply. While looking around, he could feel a calmness come over him.

Before using the gate interrupting an eight-foot-high stone wall stretching out and north from the church's north tower, Grant and McDermott wandered by the rounded front of the east end of the church, past the south tower, and stopped to take in the tall waterfall and pond. Sprinkled around the pond were three tiny gardens with benches, and a sizeable stone cross as well as a large statue of St. Paul.

"It's hard for me to fathom a better place to pray, think and read," commented Stephen.

"You're right. I did that a few times during my last stay," said Ron.

Stephen could feel his body and mind continuing to be at ease.

I didn't realize how tense I had become of late, in particular with what's going on with Sean. The sound and sight of water works every time – whether it's waves at the beach, a simple fountain, or a magnificent waterfall.

He raised his gaze up the waterfall and side of the mountain, and smiled. Stephen pulled out his phone to take a couple of photos.

Jen needs to see this.

When he went to text the images, Stephen noted that he actually had no service.

Ron interrupted, "Let's check in and see who is around."

"Okay." As they turned from the waterfall, Stephen observed, "No cell service."

Ron nodded. "Yeah, I told you that was going to be the case. When I was here last, there was nothing out here, nor in the monastery. One monk told me that they didn't want to tempt the guests or the monks with the Internet. They actually have a couple of hardline phones, so it's not the 11th century; it's the 1970s." He added, "But the store down in the village, I believe, has Internet access. After all, that's something like a business."

As they passed through the gate, Ron knew the first person to greet them. A short, roundish man with thick brown hair, matching beard, and rectangular glasses, was dressed in a plain looking dark brown monk's robe, and a rope belt. Stephen thought the man was almost a caricature of a monk, except for the white New Balance sneakers, rather than the expected brown sandals.

Ron and the monk wore broad smiles, and exchanged a hearty, back-slapping hug.

The monk declared, "Father Ron, it is wonderful to see you again."

"I'm happy to be back, Father Jules."

Hugs. Backslapping. And 'Father Ron.' Now, that's not typical for Ron.

Ron made introductions. "Father Jules DeShields, this is Pastor Stephen Grant."

As the two shook hands, DeShields said, "Ah, Pastor Stephen, welcome to our monastery."

Apparently, we're doing first names here. At St. Mary's, Stephen tended to be "Pastor Grant," while Zack was "Pastor Zack." More often than not, Grant observed, the first name or last name thing with clergy just kind of developed naturally, usually an unstated reflection of the pastor or priest's personality.

"Thank you for having me. It's a pleasure to meet you."

"I trust you'll refrain from nailing any theses to the church door."

Ah, theology humor.

"I'll try to restrain my Lutheran impulses on that front."

DeShields, who spoke English with a minor French accent, smiled and said, "Very good. Shall I give you both a tour?"

Stephen answered, "I look forward to it."

The next hour was spent covering much of the monastery's complex. Stephen was struck by the beauty of the monastery church which did, in fact, reach into the side of the mountain, as did other parts of the monastery. The church's interior created a unique atmosphere whereby the light streaming in through the stained glass windows served to help illuminate even the parts of the building carved into the mountainside.

Grant also could see the meticulous preservation and restoration work that had been done in recent decades, which seemed to capture much of what the building must have been like hundreds of years earlier. Grant noted that the interior walls were the same sand color as the exterior. He admired the entire space. While soaring and majestic, it also possessed a certain simplicity that he expected in a monastery. That went for the altar, and the massive cross suspended from the ceiling above it, at the east end, as well as the pew benches, stone floor, and choir loft built into the mountain on the west side of the space. The only items that warranted the use of the word "ornate," he thought, would be the stained glass windows running along the north and south sides of the building, capturing moments in the life of St. Paul.

Ron asked, "Father Jules, what's the latest on the tower upgrades?"

"Thank God, the north tower is completed, and we'll soon be starting on the south tower." He turned to Grant, and explained, "The towers are physically sound, but we saved the upgrades of each for the last steps in our restoration work. Would you like to go up?"

"Absolutely," responded Grant with apparent enthusiasm.

They started to climb the steps of the 70-foot tower. The staircase turned gently, and provided small sitting areas at each window on the way up. While journeying higher, looking to his left, Stephen could see all the way down to the ground. On the top floor inside the edifice, another set of stairs led up to a door. When Father Jules opened it and led them outside, Stephen slowly took in the magnificent views.

Ron said to Stephen, "And I bet you thought the views from the ground were breathtaking?"

"'Breathtaking' is the right word."

To the east was the expansive vista of parts of southern France stretching out far below.

To the north, Grant looked down on the monastery buildings. Directly next to the church was a rectangular courtyard, bordered by a covered walkway on each side that featured arches looking into the courtyard. The courtyard grass was cut into four parts by a cross of walkways.

Father Jules pointed out to Grant that the building across the courtyard was a residence hall for the monks and guests. And on the west side of the courtyard, there was a door to a chapel built into the mountain, and that also connected inside to the large church.

On the east side, the covered walkway was connected to a path from the entrance gate and the road to the complex.

Grant pointed beyond the residence building, and asked, "Where does that other door carved into the mountain lead?"

"That actually opens to stairs that go down to a complex of storage spaces, work areas, and our most secluded chapel. We use much of it these days for storage, except for the chapel."

Grant nodded.

Beyond the buildings were dark, thick green pines.

Looking west, the roof of the church stretched into the cliff, and Grant's eyes journeyed up the side of the mountain from there. And finally, a slight turn toward the south, and there again were the cool waters streaming down the side of the cliff.

Dear Lord, this is beautiful.

As they proceeded back down the stairs, Father Jules explained how the integration of various modern upgrades needed for the monks' current work were neatly hidden.

Just as they exited the church into the courtyard, a short, slim monk with narrow eyes, thin lips, small round glasses and crossed arms seemed to be waiting for them.

Father Jules smiled and said, "Ah, Father Charles, please meet two of our guests – Father Ron McDermott and Pastor Stephen Grant." He turned to Ron and Stephen, adding, "Father Charles Borget is the abbot here at our monastery."

Borget bowed slightly at the two men without unfolding his arms. He looked at Ron, and said, "Yes, I remember you from a previous visit. Welcome, Father Ron."

Ron replied, "Thank you, Father Charles."

Borget then looked at Stephen, and said, "Welcome to you as well, Pastor."

No Pastor Stephen?

Stephen said, "Thank you, Father Charles."

Borget merely said, "Yes, I have read up on you, Pastor. You have had, let us say, a colorful history."

Grant noticed Father Jules tensing up. Stephen decided to merely say, "Well, we all have our unique stories."

"Hmmm," said Borget. "I suppose. You more so than others, it would seem. After all, few have served in a place like your Central Intelligence Agency." Disapproval was apparent in Borget's tone, look and body language.

Grant responded, "I suppose not."

Borget commented, "I trust each of you will enjoy your stay." He nodded at Father Jules, and then walked by the group and into the church.

What a friendly fellow.

The three men were silent for a few seconds until Father Jules said, "I apologize." He looked at Stephen, adding, "We are not much for politics here, but Father Charles dabbles more than most, and he, unfortunately, has a less-than-favorable view of the American government."

Stephen smiled, and replied, "Apparently, Father Charles sees me as a stand in for the U.S. government. If he knew of the many problems I have with politicians, he might not be so, well, unfriendly."

Relief passed over the face of Father Jules. He said, "It takes Father Charles some time to warm up to people. Shall we continue with the tour?"

Ron interjected, "Yes, please."

As the tour proceeded, Grant came to see that the only buildings that didn't have an 11th century feel on the inside were two at the northern most part of the complex. That was where the monks worked their magic in creating a variety of chocolate truffles and bars that won over fans far and wide.

Father Jules provided Grant and McDermott a run-through on the monks' chocolate-making process.

At one point, Grant asked, "Is this the only area in your complex that has a present-day feel about it?"

Father Jules answered, "For the most part. You see, just a little farther up the road, beyond the thick pines, we have a garage and workplace for our delivery trucks. While not twenty-first century, that area is very twentieth century." Father Jules smiled. "One of our monks, Brother Hewett, is an excellent mechanic, and that very much is his domain. It seems that you can either find him in the church or in his shop, and rarely anywhere else."

Stephen and Ron nodded.

Father Jules then shifted topics. "So, gentlemen, do you have favorites among the chocolates we produce?"

Stephen sheepishly replied, "Actually, Father Jules, I've never had the chance to try your chocolates."

Father Jules seemed both shocked and excited to hear that Stephen had not yet sampled any of the monastery's delights. He showed Stephen and Ron to a small table, left briefly, and then came back with a tray of samples.

Father Jules stood smiling as Stephen took a bite of a dark chocolate Champagne-infused truffle.

Allowing the soft truffle to glide across his taste buds, Stephen began to nod his approval.

Okay, I get it. This is great.

He finished chewing and swallowing, and said, "Wow. That's incredible."

Father Jules' smile broadened – after all, he was in charge of the entire chocolate process, from creation to sales. He said "Thank you, Pastor Stephen."

Stephen replied, "No, thank you, Father Jules." He finished what remained of the truffle.

Chapter 13

It was early Friday morning, and Sean McEnany and Chase Axelrod remained in Germany much to the chagrin of Paige Caldwell. She was finishing up a call with Sean.

Caldwell said, "So, we're not any closer to figuring out where the hell Bryant is." It was a statement, not a question.

"Unfortunately," came McEnany's reply.

"It's certainly not been for a lack of trying."

McEnany said, "And I'm not going to stop trying." His tone made the statement sound like a warning.

Caldwell shot back, "No one wants to stop or said that we should stop, Sean."

He took a deep breath. "Yeah, I know. This is just extremely frustrating."

"Believe me, I get it. And I know how personal this is for you. But let's use our time and resources intelligently. You keep sweeping your contacts and resources, and the rest of us will do the same." She added, "But at the same time, we need to make sure our other clients are getting what they need."

"Yeah, yeah. I know. But there are a few avenues I still need to follow over here." He paused, and asked, "Are we leaving Chase in place to continue babysitting me?"

"I think Chase is there to help you, not babysitting."

"You could have fooled me."

"Well, if his help requires babysitting, so be it." There was another pause in their conversation. And then Caldwell added, "Do you really have a problem with Chase being there?"

McEnany's low, raspy voice lent itself to making him sound perpetually angry or annoyed. But friends and colleagues could learn to hear certain distinctions. He backed off the undertone of anger. "Of course not. Chase is always helpful."

"Good. Having him there as another set of eyes and offering insights on Bryant is probably a plus."

"It is."

Caldwell shifted gears. "When are you going to be ready to come home?"

He initially responded with silence, but then apparently decided to share his thoughts – not something McEnany did often or easily. "Every time I look at Rachel and the kids, my head goes in two different directions. After what's happened, I reflect on how blessed I am, but I also think about what happened to Ping Ho and his family. This is going to sound shitty, but it's easier to deal with Bryant while traveling. I'd like to get the job done with Bryant and Bellanger, and then come home and get back to something, well, normal."

"I understand. All I can say is that we're going to get Bryant, but I just can't tell you exactly when."

McEnany said, "I know."

"By the way, as I'm sure you are aware, Stephen's been trying to talk with you."

McEnany actually chuckled. "Is Paige Caldwell telling me to seek counseling from my pastor?"

"I wouldn't exactly put it that way. But as you know, Stephen understands all this kind of shit that we deal with. He's been through it."

"I know."

"He's actually on his way to France."

"He is?"

"Yeah, he's going on some kind of retreat at a monastery – the Monastere de Saint Paul."

"The monks with the chocolate?"

"Yes."

"Maybe I will get in contact with him. He could bring back some of their chocolate truffles for Rachel."

"He promised to bring back some for me, and you're no doubt in better with his wife than the former girlfriend from his old CIA days."

McEnany actually smiled for the first time in a while. "Thanks, Paige." He ended the call.

Chapter 14

Pastor Stephen Grant surprised himself by how quickly he became comfortable with wearing a monk's robe, and enjoying the rhythms of life at the Monastere de Saint Paul. He welcomed a growing sense of peace, and the opportunities for prayer and reflection that were uninterrupted and free from distractions.

At the same time, Grant saw firsthand how much was going on here. This monastery wasn't a place where men went into hiding. In fact, what they were doing stood in direct contrast to the temptations of leaving the outside world behind for some kind of selfish, inward focus.

That became clear on the day after Stephen and Ron arrived. They, along with two of the half-dozen other guests at the monastery, joined four of the 14 monks in residence in preparing a massive meal meant for anyone who would like to come from the Village de Saint Paul.

While receiving instructions about their visit not long after arriving, Stephen had wondered about what was listed for Saturday nights as the "Village Dinner." On the way to the kitchen on Saturday afternoon, Ron told Stephen that he should try to work with Brother Al McClay. All Ron would say is, "You should hear his story."

Brother Al was in charge of the meal's soup and salad. He was not an ordained priest – hence, the title of "Brother" rather than "Father." As Stephen discovered when they first were introduced, Brother Al was from America. Grant learned much more about the man and the monastery over the next couple of hours.

As they began work on French Country Soup, Stephen asked, "So, Brother Al, you're obviously not from France?"

The tall, thin man with short gray hair and a nose that looked to Stephen like it had been broken more than once, replied, "How did you guess? I'm from Illinois, just outside Chicago."

"Really? I'm an Ohio boy."

Brother Al shook his head, and said, "Two American Midwesterners peeling potatoes at a monastery in France."

"You never know where life is headed. So, if you don't mind me asking, what brought you to this monastery in France and how long have you been here?"

"Do you want the full story, or the abridged version?"

"Whichever you like, but we obviously have time and I've always been a good listener."

"I showed up at the gate of this place over a decade ago a bewildered and deeply ashamed man. I thought I'd find a place to go into hiding, perhaps to punish myself. I found something very different, thank God."

Stephen nodded, as the potato peeling continued.

Brother Al said, "I actually was a police officer, married with three children. I quickly became full of myself, lacking any kind of humility, even started to buy into the idea that I was better than other cops, you know, proud of taking some hits. And as my arrogance grew, I decided to have an affair with a female officer. It eventually came out, of course. I said I was sorry, and asked everyone for forgiveness. After being deeply angry and hurt, my wife and daughters truly did forgive me. It was amazing, arguably a miracle. I was given the gift of having a second chance."

"Sometimes you can just see the Holy Spirit at work in people," commented Stephen.

"You're right. Unfortunately, though, that wasn't me. I was still rejecting what God offered. I wasn't really sorry for what I had done. I was just sorry that I got caught. It's kind of ironic. I saw that sort of response in so many people I had arrested, but was blind to the fact that I was guilty of the same thing. I talked myself into why it was okay to take up the affair again, serving up excuses in my head, and that's what we did. At that point, it was all about me and saying, 'Hey, don't I deserve happiness?'"

They moved on to chopping celery, yellow onions, and garlic.

Brother Al continued to tell his story. "So, cutting out the gruesome details, I destroyed my family. My wife, well, ex-wife, has never been the same. My daughters basically despise me, and I wonder if they'll ever be able to trust a man because of what I did."

He wiped away a tear. Stephen was sure that wasn't from the onions.

The monk said, "Back then, I still didn't fully get it. I was told that I was forgiven, and that sat pretty well with me. The woman I had the affair with also left her family, and we were seeing each other publicly. We even planned on getting married, and got active in a church that was, in effect, antinomian. That, again, fit quite nicely. I think your Lutheran Dietrich Bonhoeffer called it cheap grace."

Stephen responded, "Right."

"Then we actually were being praised for what we had done. Not for the affair, but for getting active in this church after what we had done. But it felt off; kind of weird. Next, the pastor started working on a book, and it was supposed to focus on people who committed a variety of sins, and found forgiveness in Jesus. That's Good News for all of us, right?"

"Most certainly."

"But the third part of the book was to be focused on how each of these people went on to live really great lives. That's where I started to wonder about an assortment of things, specifically, what were the consequences of what I had done? I mean, here I was with this woman whom I had an affair with, everyone around us seemed really cool with all of it, and they even praised us for our journey. Our sins and the need for Christ's forgiveness were being glossed over, never mind the consequences of our sins. I mean nobody seemed to care what had happened to my wife, my daughters, or the family of my partner in the affair. The more I thought about it, the more uncomfortable I became. And what would being part of this book mean to my wife and daughters? Wouldn't it be like rubbing their noses in what I had done? And was this going to help them in their lives and relationships with God? But no one liked these questions – not the pastor, not the woman I was with, and not many church members. My wife – well, again, ex-wife – wanted nothing to do with me, and I couldn't lay more of what I had done on my daughters. I was completely alone, and had no idea what to do."

Brother Al paused, and looked at Stephen. "I haven't talked about this in some time."

"Are you sure you want to?"

"I do. Are you sure you want to continue hearing it?"

"If this is helping you, Brother Al, then please continue."

"Alright, thanks. I continued working for another year or so until I hit my 20 years. I retired, and withdrew from most everything in my life. I wound up staying home a great deal, and started reading the Bible and assorted Catholic writers. I found myself attending Mass fairly regularly. But I still was adrift. And then at one of our church's fundraisers, I won a box of chocolate truffles from this place – the Monastere de Saint Paul. I ate these delicious creations and did a little research on who these monks were. And I can't explain it fully, but I arranged for my pension to be sent to my ex-wife, I sold almost everything I had, got on a plane, and showed up here."

"Wow. Just like that?"

Al nodded. "And while here this past decade or so, I learned some important things."

"And those are?" asked Stephen.

"I came to understand what St. Paul wrote, 'For there is no distinction: for all have sinned and fall short of the glory of God, and are justified by his grace as a gift, through the redemption that is in Christ Jesus, whom God put forward as a propitiation by his blood, to be received by faith.'"

Grant could not resist. "Lutherans love that passage."

"I understand why. But that doesn't mean that we get to keep on sinning. After all, Jesus did say to the woman who committed adultery, 'Neither do I condemn you; go, and from now on sin no more.' So, God's grace is not an excuse to sin, to ignore the Ten Commandments, for example, to assume there are no consequences to our sins on this earth. So, while I have repented and am forgiven, that doesn't mean that I don't have to take responsibility for my actions in the here and now."

"All true," added Grant.

"I suppose like everyone else, I continue to struggle with my sins and with their consequences. And I sometimes wonder if, in fact, part of me is in hiding here at St. Paul's." He paused, but then continued. "I think about St. James going along with St. Paul. As you know, James wrote that 'faith by itself, if it does not have works, is dead.' I know this has long been debated in the Church, for centuries, by much bigger minds than mine. I just simply look at it as my faith requires things of me. I try, then, to do better. I've gone home a few times, and reached out to my ex-wife and my daughters. I try to figure out what might actually help, as opposed to what could make things worse. I have to work at that. I was never much good at sorting those kinds of things out. You know, what's really going to help others and what's really just about me?"

Grant added, "You most certainly are not alone in trying to figure that out."

"I think my work here helps others – my fellow monks, the locals and our guests. And hey, maybe there's someone out there who had an experience, or will have an experience like mine when it comes to trying a piece of our chocolate."

Grant commented, "You're wrestling with the things that we all do on various levels – absent the chocolate, for the most part."

Brother Al smiled, and added, "Perhaps with less success."

"Don't believe that, Brother Al. All of us have to take responsibility for our actions, work to do better, and at the same time, realize that we ultimately rely on Christ crucified and resurrected."

It was Brother Al's turn to nod in agreement. He added, "For what it's worth, if you haven't noticed, at various places throughout the monastery, you'll see signs or plaques with 1 Thessalonians 5:12-18 written on them. It's like a motto around here. It helps me to keep things in perspective."

He pointed to a sign hanging above one of the doorways.

Brother Al asked, "How's your French?"

"Rusty would be generous."

So, Brother Al read it aloud:

> "We ask you, brothers, to respect those who labor among you and are over you in the Lord and admonish you, and to esteem them very highly in love because of their work. Be at peace among yourselves. And we urge you, brothers, admonish the idle, encourage the fainthearted, help the weak, be patient with them all. See that no one repays anyone evil for evil, but always seek to do good to one another and to everyone. Rejoice always, pray without ceasing, give thanks in all circumstances; for this is the will of God in Christ Jesus for you."
> - 1 Thessalonians 5:12-18

Grant simply said, "Good stuff. I love that."

As they proceeded with making soup and then salad, the two men spoke more about the work of the monks beyond being chocolatiers, including visiting shut-ins and hospitals, helping out various churches in the region when needed, and always having their doors open for people to join in the various services offered each day.

Grant reflected that in key ways, the monastery functioned as many local parishes do. He also gave Brother Al a rundown on his own background, from growing up in the Cincinnati area to the SEALs and CIA, and finally to becoming a pastor.

Brother Al summed up, "Now that is one of the more unique paths I've heard to becoming a member of the clergy."

It was clear that Brother Al's law enforcement background, and Stephen's SEAL and CIA service, worked to create a further bond between the two men.

That Saturday night's dinner brought in almost 30 people in addition to the monks and monastery guests. Both Ron McDermott and Stephen Grant were glad to attend what turned out to be part dinner and part celebration. Like the monastery itself and the monks who lived, prayed and worked there, a simple joy and authenticity was evident in the entire event.

Grant noted that the abbot, Father Charles, was warm and welcoming to everyone – and even appeared to be a little less icy toward Stephen himself.

Chapter 15

The cab of the delivery truck offered a bench for seating three. Behind the wheel was Father Jules DeShields, with Father Ron McDermott in the middle and Pastor Stephen Grant on the other side.

Ron said, "That was fascinating."

"How so?" asked Jules.

"Delivering chocolate to these stores turned out to be an opportunity to talk about Christ and his Church. That was unexpected."

It was mid-Tuesday afternoon, and the three men had just completed deliveries to six shops over several hours. The truck was now making the ascent back up to the Village de Saint Paul.

Stephen added, "I agree. Your relationships with the store owners and workers were much more than merely as a supplier. They clearly spoke with you in ways and about things they wouldn't with other business partners."

Jules responded, "I suppose that is true. I never thought of it in those specific terms – I mean in comparison to how they might interact with other suppliers. This is just what we do."

Stephen replied, "I like that: 'This is just what we do.' Plus, food tends to work in getting people to church, so serving up some of the most delicious chocolate on the continent can't hurt."

Jules and Ron laughed.

Stephen continued, "On a different matter, I have to say that I was a bit taken off guard by your sneakers when we first met."

Father Jules replied, "Yes, most people are."

"But after going on these deliveries, I get why you wear them. These sandals" – Stephen pointed to what he had on – "don't really work for making chocolate deliveries."

Jules agreed, "The sneakers, while not fitting with the robe, do allow me to work more efficiently. Besides, the sandals also are difficult on my back."

Ron added, "I understand that."

As the small truck entered the village, Jules remarked, "I need to stop at the shop before we head up to the monastery."

Jules went to make a right just before reaching the monastery's store in order to park around back. While turning, Grant spotted a large, silver SUV parked on the street near the chocolate shop. The vehicle stood out on the stone road, especially given that the sprinkling of other vehicles in the area were either small cars or related to farming.

Father Jules parked the truck behind the store, and the three men entered via a back entrance. That took them into a small office and adjacent storage room. Jules stopped in the office, along with Ron. Stephen decided to continue moving toward the store area in response to hearing Brother Al's voice. But as he took a few steps forward, Grant felt a kind of tightness – like pressure building up – in his head and ears. It was a feeling that came upon him when danger lurked. He called it a "red alert," and since his days as a SEAL and with the CIA, Grant knew not to ignore a red alert.

Stephen pulled aside the curtain separating the two areas, and stepped forward.

Grant initially saw the back of Brother Al's dark brown robe. The monk was speaking amiably with a customer, who was wearing sunglasses.

Sunglasses in a small, relatively low-lit store on a cloudy fall day?

Two large men lurked behind the individual with sunglasses. They stood unmoving – one looking out the front window of the shop and the other keeping an eye on the man obviously being guarded and Brother Al.

Brother Al turned, smiled and said, "Pastor Stephen, how did the deliveries go?"

"They went well. How are you?"

"Well, thanks." Al turned back to his customer.

When the man removed his sunglasses, Grant was hit hard. He immediately recognized the individual. Stephen fought to make sure he showed no reaction. His mind raced.

Shorter hair and the addition of a beard, but no doubts. Hunter Bryant. Holy shit. Worldwide manhunt and this asshole walks into the monks' chocolate shop. At least three-dozen people are dead because of him. If he leaves this store and gets in that SUV, the process of tracking this murderer and traitor starts all over again. Can't let that happen. Options? Two bodyguards in here, and someone driving the SUV. I have no weapons, and two monks and a priest to worry about.

Part of Grant's brain was listening to the conversation between Bryant and Al.

He's actually talking about how he can have chocolates shipped to his mother in the U.S. Even traitors love these truffles?

Grant returned to the challenge at hand.

Can't trust the French to help, or any other authorities in Europe. They either love Bellanger and this guy, or they don't want to piss off those who do. I also can't exactly follow them in a delivery truck.

Grant took in the details of what lay before him once more.

The two guards are armed – shoulder holsters under their jackets. Okay. Start with the SUV and move back from there.

Grant turned and stepped back behind the curtain. He spoke loudly, "Father Ron."

Ron McDermott stuck his head out from the office.

Grant spoke so all could hear once more, "I'm going across the street for a coffee. Anyone want one?"

Father Jules called out, "No, thank you," from inside the office. Ron added, "No, thanks." But when he looked at Stephen's face, Ron started to say more.

Stephen, however, held up a finger to his own lips, signaling his friend to be quiet. He then mouthed in silence, "Stay in the office."

Ron froze with a concerned look.

Grant pointed, indicating for him to go back into the office. As Ron did so, Stephen turned and went back through the curtain. He looked at Al, "And you, Brother Al?"

"No, thank you."

As Grant moved toward the shop's door, he double checked everything.

Definitely Bryant. Both guards armed.

He said, "Excuse me," while passing each of the two guards.

Stephen exited the store. The SUV was parked several yards up the road from the shop. As he walked toward the vehicle, Grant was trying to figure out if the SUV was beyond the view of the guard who was looking out the chocolate shop's small front window. Grant believed it was, but he wasn't completely sure.

A couple entered the coffee shop farther up the road, so now the street was empty but for Grant and his target.

Well, if things go sideways, they'll come at me, and leave Ron and the monks alone.

Grant smiled. While approaching the driver's window, he made a demonstration of looking at the SUV. The driver lowered his window, and asked, "Is there something I can help you with, Father?"

Grant could understand and speak French, to a very limited extent. He decided to respond in English, in part, to further distract the driver – whether the man could speak English or not.

"I'm just fascinated by your SUV."

The driver failed to smile with Grant.

Grant continued, "I mean I'm an American. And I love these things. But I've been at this monastery in France for so long that seeing a nice big vehicle like this is pretty rare." He leaned in closer to the window, and lowered his voice. "You know, those European cars are all so small."

Grant spotted the holstered weapon.

Suppressor attached. Good, if necessary.

"Yes, well...," the driver started.

English, okay.

Grant repositioned himself. "The inside is nice, too."

The driver said, "Father, if you could please..."

Grant mustered as much strength and speed as possible as he drove his fist into the side of the man's face. He assumed the punch wouldn't be enough to deliver the driver into unconsciousness. Grant's hope was to daze the man, grab the gun, and use the butt to knock him out. But that's not the way it played out.

The driver turned out to be less affected by the punch than Grant had expected. But Stephen did reach the gun before the driver did. As the man's hand grabbed Grant's with the gun, the driver actually had an advantage. Both men were righthanded. Grant's left hand grasped the pistol, which was still halfway in the holster. The driver's right hand was over Grant's and the gun. In addition, the driver was grounded in his seat, while Grant had to balance half hanging on and reaching into the car window.

The struggle was fully engaged in a tiny space, with Grant partially on top of the driver. Their heads banged together. Grant could feel the other man's perspiration, and hear grunting that was silent to the rest of the world.

The driver reached up with his left hand, grabbed a chunk of Grant's black hair, and started pulling. But Grant didn't use his free right hand to respond to that action. Instead, Grant grabbed the side of the driver's head, and drove his thumb into the man's left eye.

The pain and surprise resulted in Hunter Bryant's driver loosening his grip in the struggle for the pistol. Grant pulled the gun completely out of its holster, turned the barrel into his opponent's chest, and pulled the trigger twice.

The driver whispered, "No..." His body went limp, and Grant pulled himself out of the car window. He looked around.

No one on the street still.

As he moved quickly back toward the chocolate shop, Grant noted that no one was yet emerging from the store. He folded his arms, hiding the gun inside the wide sleeves of his robe. The one thing that Grant initially failed to notice was that the driver's blood had sprayed on the front of his robe. But as he reached down to open the front door of the store, Grant spotted the blood.

Oh, crap.

He continued to open the door and started to step inside.

The guard looking out the front window immediately saw the blood on Grant's robe, and began to pull out his own gun.

Grant resigned himself to what had to now happen.

God, help me and forgive me.

He was able to move far more quickly than his opposition. Stephen slipped the gun out from under his sleeve. He pointed the pistol at the guard's head, and pulled the trigger. Blood, and pieces of flesh and skull splattered, and the man crashed back into a display of chocolate bars.

The second guard spun, and almost had his gun in a position to fire when Grant's second shot entered his chest. The man slammed into the shop's counter, and slid to the floor.

After turning, Hunter Bryant had watched this play out while standing frozen.

Brother Al actually stood without moving as well, with his hands held out in the air in front of him.

Grant moved forward and grabbed Bryant. "Are you armed?"

Bryant was unresponsive. He merely looked at Grant in a kind of shock.

Grant pushed him against a large, heavy wooden case filled with assorted packaged truffles. Grant searched

Bryant and found no weapons, but pulled out a wallet, money clip, and two cellphones. While doing so, Grant said over his shoulder, "Brother Al, this is Hunter Bryant. He's a traitor, and his actions got people killed and tortured."

Al merely replied, "Okay."

"I need you to put your hands down, snap out of it, go outside, and drive that silver SUV around to the back of the store."

"Um, alright." But Brother Al still failed to move.

Grant turned and looked at the monk. "Al. You were a cop once. I need you to be one again for a few minutes. Move the SUV now."

"But what are you doing? Who are you, really?"

Grant said, "I told you who I am, and that I'd worked with the CIA."

Brother Al raised his eyebrows. But then he moved around the counter and the dead body up against it.

Grant added, "The driver's dead. You're going to have to slide him out of the way."

Brother Al merely nodded as he proceeded.

Grant turned Bryant around, and said, "You're going to be dealt with appropriately."

Bryant's eyes moved up and down Grant. "What the hell? You're a fucking monk."

Grant replied, "More like a warrior monk."

"You'll pay for this."

"No, that's what you're going to do." Anger washed over Grant. "Let me clue you in, Bryant. You're going to die one way or another. If you try anything before I hand you over to the right authorities, I'm more than willing to dispense justice. And trust me, you'll have a better chance in the U.S. justice system. But even with the best lawyers, you're still going to pay the ultimate price for being a traitor and sending good people to their deaths."

"If they worked with the U.S., then they weren't any good."

Grant restrained himself from slapping Bryant across the face with the gun in his hand. He did say, "You're just a little shit, aren't you?"

It was clear that for Hunter Bryant anger was now crowding out fear. "And you just said that you were with the CIA? I know firsthand what a piece of shit you are then."

For another moment, the pastor inside Grant took a step back, and let the former CIA operative act. Grant swung the butt of the gun into the side of Bryant's face. The man crashed to the floor.

Grant immediately regretted doing that. He reached down, grabbed the back of Bryant's shirt, and pulled him up to his feet.

Ron and Jules emerged slowly from behind the curtain. The two looked at the dead men on the floor, and then at Grant. Jules blessed himself.

Stephen gave them the quick rundown on what happened and who the man was that he was holding at gunpoint. He then looked at Jules and said, "Phone?"

Jules blankly responded, "We don't get any service up here."

"Yes, I know. The landline."

Jules seemed to push aside his bewilderment. "Oh, yes. It's in the office."

Brother Al then returned, coming out from behind the curtain. "The SUV is in the back."

Grant looked at the three men, each displaying varying degrees of disbelief, fear and disgust. "I have to ask you for more help."

Ron immediately replied, "What do you need, Stephen?"

"While I take Bryant with me into the office to make a call so someone can come get him – and these two and the guy in the SUV..."

Jules said, "Guy in the SUV?"

Grant chose to ignore that and continued, "I'll call for help, but I need you to lock the front door, pull down the shades, move these two into the back of the SUV, and clean up in here."

The three looked around mystified. Ron then said, "Yes, yes, we'll get that done."

Grant looked at all three, and asked, "Are you all sure?" The three nodded.

Grant added, "Oh, and please make sure any cellphones or other electronics on these guys are turned off."

Ron answered, "Okay."

Grant pushed Bryant into the back office, and shoved him into a chair. While keeping the gun trained on his prisoner, Grant dialed a number from memory.

The voice on the other end answered, "Yes, who is this?"

"Sean, this is Stephen."

After a brief hesitation, Sean McEnany started to reply, "Stephen, listen, I'm sorry..."

Grant interrupted, "No time for that. We'll have a heart to heart soon enough. Are you still in Germany?"

"Yes, with Chase."

"Good. You two need to get to France right now."

"Why?"

"Because I'm sitting in a French chocolate shop owned by monks, with a gun pointed at Hunter Bryant."

Chapter 16

Alessia Rossi did knock, but chose not to wait for an acknowledgement before entering Garth Bellanger's office in his estate outside of Paris. On the journey to his desk, Rossi shifted back and forth between jogging and walking quickly.

While holding a smartphone out in her right hand, she called, "Garth, Garth, Hunter has sent an emergency signal!"

Bellanger stood up, and said, "What?"

As she started to close in on the desk, Rossi declared, "We have an emergency signal from Hunter, as well as from one of the guards. However, neither one has responded to the follow-up messages. They are not following protocol. No one in the group is responding."

Bellanger said, "Shit." He grabbed his own smartphone that had been resting on the desk, and proceeded to try contacting Bryant and each of the security detail.

Rossi stood waiting for instructions.

Bellanger asked, "What about their locations?"

"I have where they were when the emergency messages were sent. However, the phones have now gone dark."

"What about the tracker in the SUV?"

She shook her head. "It also is no longer transmitting."

"Nothing on the news, right?"

Rossi confirmed, "Nothing."

"Where did they go off the grid – in France?"

"Yes. A location in the southeast, in the Alps."

Bellanger said, "Check with our French law enforcement contacts. Do it quietly and do not volunteer anything. Just see if they have anything to tell us."

"Yes, sir," she replied. Rossi then turned and started the trek back to the door.

Bellanger cursed, once again, and then hit a button on his desk phone.

A response came from the speaker, "Yes, sir?"

Bellanger ordered, "Get Blade and Leach in here, now!"

"Of course," replied the voice.

When the office door opened, Rossi stepped out and the two leaders of Bellanger's personal guards entered. Marvin Blade and Russell Leach quickly covered the space to their boss's desk. As usual, the two men wore dark shirts and suits. Each had body-builder, six-foot frames, square heads and short dark hair. Both also were Americans and former-military-turned-mercenary bodyguards. It seemed that the only difference between the two was that Blade was black and Leach was white.

Blade merely said, "Yes, sir."

"We have a problem. Emergency signals came from Bryant and one of his guards. However, that was it. They have gone dark."

The two men nodded while listening.

Bellanger continued, "Rossi has the location. Put two teams together, get Bryant, and clean up any problems." He paused and looked closely at each man. "Don't leave any loose ends."

"Yes, sir."

Chapter 17

As Sean McEnany finished the call with Stephen Grant, Chase Axelrod entered the room. Axelrod asked, "What was that about?"

"Grant has captured Hunter Bryant."

"What!? Where? How?"

McEnany went on to relay what Stephen had told him, including the fact that Bryant's three-man security team was dead and that Grant was about to hide Bryant in a monastery in southern France.

Axelrod shook his head, and said, "Holy shit."

McEnany said, "I told Grant that we'd leave here immediately to get Bryant. Grab what we need, and let's move."

"Right, but first, let's tell Paige what's going on. Maybe she can get us – get Stephen – more help."

McEnany reacted, "*I* want Bryant."

Axelrod replied, "Sean, we all want Bryant. We want to make sure we do this using our heads. What's the fastest way to secure Bryant?"

"We need people who can be trusted on this. Who the hell is that other than us?"

Axelrod looked at his friend, and said in a calming voice, "Sean, just call Paige, and we can go from there."

McEnany reluctantly acquiesced. Caldwell answered and McEnany proceeded to rapidly fire the details of what had occurred.

Caldwell took a moment to say, "How does Stephen do it? Maybe he does have a special deal with God."

"Paige." McEnany's voice was drenched in impatience.

"Right. You just might be on your own. But let's hope not. I'll call Tank and get right back to you."

"Okay. But no wasted time."

Caldwell replied with an edge. "Yeah, I know what the situation is, Sean." She ended the call.

Ten minutes later, McEnany's phone barely had a chance to ring. He immediately answered, "Okay, Paige, what's the story?"

"Tank is leaving this to us, and therefore, to you two."

"Alright, so we're going to..."

"Hold on. He is making sure, however, that you have access to transportation and tools of the trade. There will be a Learjet waiting for you at the Munich Airport. Two friends of the Agency will fly you to the Avignon Airport, and waiting for you there will be a vehicle and the necessary equipment to secure Bryant, and if needed, fend off any of Bellanger's goons."

McEnany's tone softened somewhat. "That's great."

"In addition, we take off from here within the hour. If everything goes smoothly, we'll return Bryant to the U.S. on our own plane."

The two exchanged additional details, and Caldwell said, "Good luck. We'll see you soon."

"Thanks, Paige."

After the call ended, McEnany said to Axelrod, "Tank came through with a plane, and a vehicle and weapons on the other end."

"Good," replied Axelrod. "Who knows if Bellanger is sending someone to find Bryant? We might need some extra firepower."

Chapter 18

While Sean was talking with Chase and Paige, McDermott was driving the SUV and following the monks' delivery truck up the tight, winding road toward the monastery. Grant was in the back seat, keeping a gun trained on Bryant. In the third row of the SUV were the bodies of the three men assigned by Garth Bellanger to protect Hunter Bryant. And in the very back of the SUV were an assortment of weapons and equipment that Grant expected a security team like Bryant's would have.

Best case scenario: Sean and Chase get here before Bellanger and his people do. No, the best case is that Bellanger has no clue what's going on, and none of his people are on the way. But understanding who these people are, I doubt that's the case.

Grant mentally sighed to himself. And to make sure nothing was missed, he also reviewed in his mind what he had done before the SUV rolled, including making sure that all cellphone and communication devices, including the tracker in the SUV, were inoperable.

Worst case: Bellanger's people get here first and this turns ugly. No. Not acceptable. Bad-but-not-worst case: I now have the weapons and the place of my choosing to defend against any hostiles.

And then the larger problem hit him.

What the hell do I do with the monks and their guests? Crap.

The truck and SUV went past the monastery church and adjacent buildings, and through another patch of pines.

Moving beyond the trees, Grant saw the garage area that Father Jules had mentioned during their arrival tour and the place that he suggested would work for hiding the SUV, not to mention the bodies inside the vehicle.

There were two buildings up against the cliff. The first was a small structure that served as an office and a storage facility for parts, tools and so on. The second was a long building with five bays. But what focused Grant's attention was a coach bus parked on the other side of the garage. "Le Choclat de le Monastere de Saint Paul," along with pictures of various chocolate products from the monks, were spread across the sides of the bus.

Grant asked, "What the hell is that?"

Ron replied, "The monastery has a bus for various day trips for guests."

Grant declared, "I want everyone on that bus and out of here within an hour."

"What?"

"Trust me, Ron."

Delivery trucks were parked in the first two garage bays. Father Jules pulled his truck into the third, and McDermott, as instructed by Father Jules before they left the store in the village, backed the SUV into the fourth bay.

After exiting the vehicles, Father Jules and Ron moved to close all five of the garage doors. At the same time, Brother Al, who had been riding with Jules in the truck, made his way toward the side door of the building. But before he reached it, the door opened, and in stepped a man in a dark blue jumpsuit. He was on the heavy side, and had red hair and a matching beard, mixed with bits of gray.

The man had a soft voice. "Brother Al, what are you doing to my garage?"

Brother Al McClay replied, "We have an emergency, Brother Hewett."

"What is happening?"

Father Jules stepped forward. As he explained what had happened, Jules periodically pointed to the SUV. While listening, Hewett's mouth slowly widened in amazement.

McDermott walked up to the group, and Father Jules introduced Ron to Hewett. The two men shook hands.

McDermott asked, "Brother Hewett, is your bus ready to roll?"

Hewett looked more bewildered, and spoke barely above a whisper, "What? The bus? Yes, why?"

Ron looked at the three monks of the Monastere de Saint Paul, and said, "You need to get everyone in the monastery on that bus and away from here."

Father Jules replied, "Excuse me?"

McDermott continued, "And it needs to happen within the hour."

Father Jules and Brother Hewett stood in silence. Jules rubbed his chin, and finally said, "Stephen wants this done?"

"Yes," answered McDermott.

"I understand why." He stood up a bit straighter, and added, "Father Charles is going to be a problem, but I will make it very clear to him why this must happen. Everyone will go whether Father Charles likes it or not."

Grant waited impatiently and silently with Bryant in the SUV. Bryant merely stared straight ahead, with his hands bound together by a zip tie that Grant had found among a variety of equipment, tools and weapons in the vehicle. Grant's eyes moved back and forth between Bryant and the spot in front of the delivery truck where someone would return from the conversation occurring at the other end of the long garage, hidden from Grant's current view.

Finally, McDermott came around the corner. He opened the driver's door and leaned in, glancing with some disgust at Bryant. He said, "The bus is ready to go. Brother Hewett, who runs this garage, is going to drive it down to the front gate of the monastery. Father Jules and Brother Al are going to make sure everyone gets on it. But Father Charles might be a problem."

Bryant smiled, looked at Grant, and said, "You should leave, too, or you're going to pay a big price."

Anger surged inside Grant. He pushed the gun up against the side of Bryant's head, and said, "If I want to hear anything from you, I'll ask first."

Ron simply said, "Stephen."

Grant slowly lowered the gun and turned his gaze away from Bryant.

Ron asked, "What's next?"

Chapter 19

Marvin Blade and Russell Leach led six other individuals – all dressed in black combat attire – across an expansive lawn adjacent to Garth Bellanger's sprawling residence. They were walking toward an Airbus H215M helicopter.

Like Blade and Leach, the other six were sizeable and ex-military who had been hired by Bellanger as part of his security team. While Blade and Leach were Americans, three under their command on this day were from France, two from Russia and one was Egyptian.

As they walked, Blade and Leach were finishing up the rundown on the mission.

Blade stopped in the field, and turned to look at the six. "We're not exactly sure what we're heading into, including if Bryant and his team are still in this last-known area or if they're even still alive. In my opinion, if Bryant was grabbed and is still alive, I don't expect that we're going to find him in the area. If Bryant and his guards were taken down, then it had to be by a team that knew what they were doing. If I'm right, we gather evidence, find out who took Bryant, where they're headed, and track them down. If I'm wrong, we get Bryant back, and leave nothing and no one behind that could cause problems. Everyone okay with that?"

Blade received positive responses from everyone around him.

"Good. When we touch down, there will be two vehicles waiting for us. As usual, they will be fully stocked with everything needed. The drive to the village will be less than 15 minutes. Any questions?"

Leach and the six were silent.

Blade said, "Okay, then, let's get Bellanger's boy back."

The eight then trotted toward the helicopter, and climbed on board.

Thumbs-up gave confirmation all around, and the copter lifted off, rose in the air, and began its journey south. The flight was scheduled to take less than two-and-a-half hours.

Chapter 20

Forty-five minutes had passed when Hunter Bryant emerged from the small side door of the long garage followed by Stephen Grant. Bryant's hands were still bound, while Grant still held a gun in his right hand.

Grant directed Bryant toward a pathway cut through the large patch of pine trees.

Grant decided it was time to delve into the thinking and motivations of Bryant. "Your family must be very proud."

Bryant replied over his shoulder, "Fuck you."

Grant ignored the comment, and continued, "I mean, a father who is a retired colonel in the Army. And then there's your mom, who works with the Air Force, a brother in the Navy and a sister who is an FBI special agent. And you sign up with the CIA. What happened to turn you into a traitor?"

"I'm no traitor. My country became the traitor."

The two men entered the pines.

Grant asked, "Please, Bryant, illuminate me?"

"I don't think that's possible."

"Try."

An arrogance entered his voice. "The United States has been the source of most of the world's problems. If we'd simply minded our own business, things would be much better." He paused, and in a slightly lower voice, Bryant added, "And there would be fewer senseless deaths."

That last point sounded personal.

Grant replied, "I can't tell you how many times I've heard such naïve drivel. It comes from various corners, such as populists, the Left, libertarians, isolationists on the Right, and so on. Where do you fit in?"

"I'm not naïve, and I'm not about any of those groups. I just understand the evil that America has done."

"I'll agree that the U.S. isn't perfect or without sin. None of us are. But what about stopping the Nazis in World War II, working to combat, contain and yes, eventually defeat communism in the Cold War, doing battle with a violent, radical Islamic fascism, and playing the key role in spreading freedom and prosperity? You know, thanks to our Declaration of Independence and Constitution, and free enterprise and trade. That's not too shabby."

Bryant merely responded, "If you believe such lies."

"What about us protecting the South Koreans? Look at the difference between the poverty and horrors of North Korea and what has happened in South Korea."

In a low, steely tone, Bryant replied, "Don't ever bring up what the U.S. has done in Korea."

They emerged from the pines, and proceeded through a side gate in the monastery wall.

Grant directed Bryant around a building. "And what about the people who died because you stole top secret information, and you and Bellanger handed it over to the Chinese?"

Not too far in the distance, Grant heard an engine rev up and the coach bus start to pull away.

"No one died because of what I or Garth did. Nothing was handed over to the Chinese. Those are lies, propaganda. Most of the information that I liberated has been released to the public, to the people who have a right to know, and the rest will be released after Garth confirms that no one could be hurt by doing so."

Grant responded, "Now, who is buying into lies? Do you tell yourself this in order to sleep?"

Bryant whirled around in anger.

Grant smirked. "What are you going to do, Hunter?" Grant looked at Bryant's tied hands, and then at the gun in his own hand. Grant decided to press. "So, your parents, your brother and your sister are just idiots, dupes? Or is there something else at work here? What's the real reason that you're lying to yourself?"

Grant was a bit surprised when Bryant screamed, and started to run at him, reaching out with his bound hands. Grant took a quick step to the side. He extended his right leg, and pushed Bryant with his left hand. As a result, Bryant lost his balance, tripping over Grant's leg and crashing down onto the stone walkway.

A voice came from behind Grant. "What is happening here?"

Grant turned quickly, pointing his gun. He immediately lowered the weapon upon seeing Father Charles Borget, with Ron and Brother Al standing behind him.

Grant said, "What are you three still doing here?"

Ron started to say, "I'm sorry, Stephen, but..."

Borget interrupted, "This is *my* monastery. You're the one who needs to answer questions. I have been told what you've done, Pastor Grant, and I am shocked and appalled."

While Grant turned his eyes back to Bryant, he spoke over his shoulder to Borget. "I understand, Father Charles. But you must realize what this man has done. Some of it has been reported, but..."

Borget interrupted, "What I have heard about is a man who is interested in transparency, not secrecy. He has worked to expose the duplicity of your country."

Lord, help me, please.

"Is that why you allowed your guests and most of the monks" – he looked over Borget's shoulder at Ron, who nodded – "to leave on that bus? Because Mr. Bryant and his friend, Garth Bellanger, are just a couple of good guys interested in exposing wrongdoing? Or would it be because you see the possibility that Bellanger might be sending thugs to kill anyone trying to bring Hunter Bryant to justice for his crimes?"

Borget countered, "You mean like you apparently murdered Mr. Bryant's guards?"

Grant sighed. "Before I make preparations for a possible attack by Mr. Bryant's friends, I'm going to take a few minutes to briefly educate you, and apparently, Mr. Bryant, about the reality of what came about due to his stealing top secret information about individuals who were fighting against totalitarianism in China and North Korea." Without providing names, Grant explained what he knew about the individuals who had been murdered.

Grant could see evidence of some realization developing on Borget's face. That was not the case with Bryant, however, whose expression remained stoic.

Grant concluded, "That's all I have time for right now. I'd be glad to further debate the matter after Bryant here has been secured, and we're sure that we're out of danger." He looked at Ron and Brother Al, and said, "Since you're still here, can I ask you for some help?"

Ron replied, "Of course."

Brother Al glanced at Borget, who now stood motionless. Al then looked at Grant and nodded.

Grant pushed Bryant by Borget, and Ron and Brother Al fell in next to Stephen. Borget turned and followed, walking with his head down.

Grant spoke to Brother Al. "I know the south tower of the church is closed to the public and it hasn't been upgraded yet. Is it usable, however?"

"Usable?"

"Yes, can we get up the stairs and onto the turret?"

"Yes."

"Good."

Grant was soon pushing Bryant along across the courtyard, and into the church. Grant asked Brother Al to unlock the door to the south tower. Stephen leaned through the door to take a look. "Any electricity in here?"

"No. Not yet," replied Brother Al.

Ron then asked, "Why the tower, Stephen?"

"Limited access, and we'd have the high ground."

Ron smiled shakily, and said, "The high ground. Just like Sam Elliott in *Gettysburg*."

Grant nodded. "He played General John Buford, with a great voice for the role. Yes, Sam Elliott was right to want the high ground."

Grant turned to Brother Al. "Can I ask you to bring the old cop out again?"

"What do you need me to do?"

"Take this gun and guard Bryant, while Ron and I retrieve some equipment from the SUV."

Brother Al took the gun, and said, "Sure, no problem."

Grant said, "Thanks."

Al turned to Bryant, pointed the weapon, and said, "Let's go take a seat on one of the pews. I think you could use some quiet prayer time."

Grant watched as Brother Al moved behind Bryant. He also noted that Borget remained quiet and moved along with Brother Al.

Grant said to Ron, "Come on, let's go."

"Okay. What are we bringing back?"

"Almost anything we can fight and protect ourselves with, and from what I could see, we'll have a respectable arsenal to rely on, if needed."

Chapter 21

As he moved, and distributed weapons and tools with Ron's help, Stephen felt an uncomfortable unease that hadn't plagued him in a very long time. In fact, this was a specific unease that he had felt only on the rarest of occasions even during his SEAL and CIA days. It came from not being able to get a handle on what might lie just ahead, and not being able to make a reasonable assessment of possible scenarios.

He recalled a conversation with Jennifer, as he took some time to lounge in her office while she was working one afternoon. She wound up providing a quick economist lesson on the difference between "risk" and "uncertainty." She said, "Most people see the two words as interchangeable, but in reality, the differences are substantial. Risk means that you can predict the possibility of future outcomes; so, risk can be measured and managed. But uncertainty can't be predicted in any way and it can't be measured, so it's uncontrollable."

He enjoyed the brief moment of thinking about his wife. And then Stephen occupied part of his mind with a debate as to whether he was dealing with risk or uncertainty in the current situation.

I have to assume that Bryant or one of his guards managed to send some kind of signal to Bellanger that there was trouble. And I have to assume that a Bellanger team is going to get here before Sean and Chase. But I don't really have a clue on any of that. In our favor, they don't know exactly where we are.

He looked over at Ron who was dutifully following Stephen's instructions.

And I'm not on my own now. I have to worry about Ron, not to mention Brother Al and Father Charles. Can I expect any real help from either Ron or Al if things get hot? Dear Lord, please be with all of us, and help me to make the right choices. Right choices? Should I have even brought Bryant back here?

Stephen and Ron allocated semiautomatic handguns and rifles, and accompanying magazines, two small cases with nine grenades in each, and other equipment between the turrets atop the two church towers.

Grant assigned Ron, Brother Al and Father Charles to the north tower, with instructions to be ready but to remain quiet, stay low, and limit movements. Ron and Al agreed, but Borget refused to go with them. He declared, "I will be staying with you and Mr. Bryant." Grant couldn't dissuade him, and didn't want to waste time trying.

So, on the top of the south tower sat Bryant, with hands still bound, Father Charles Borget and Stephen Grant.

Darkness began to set in, and the clouds from earlier in the day cleared out. Grant looked around and took note of some of the differences between the refurbished north tower and the decay of where he now sat with Bryant and Borget. Various stones were loose and crumbling, and the wall around the turret was far lower than on the north tower. He didn't necessarily mind that, as it provided him with a better view of the ground.

Grant positioned himself so that he could keep an eye on Bryant while also watching the road approaching the monastery. Borget sat across the circular space from both Bryant and Grant. The three men's relative positions formed a triangle.

From where Grant sat, he had a perfect view beyond Bryant of the waterfall streaming down the side of the mountain. The sight and sound of the water served as striking contrasts to the entire situation now playing out before Grant.

Borget looked at Grant and, barely above a whisper, said, "If it is true what you said, then I understand that what Mr. Bryant and Mr. Bellanger did was wrong. Although, I'm not sure that they understood or intended the outcomes."

Grant shook his head.

Borget asked, "What is it? Why do you shake your head?"

"I've never understood my fellow clergy members who insist upon assuming the best – even when confronted by evidence to the contrary or with evidence of outright evil being done."

"As a priest, I think I'm supposed to assume the best about people."

"Really? That's an interesting take on human nature."

"Human nature is fundamentally good."

Grant replied, "Hmmm, Saint Paul might disagree."

Borget argued, "So, you assume and expect the worst from everyone?"

"Quite the contrary, I've learned to assume nothing, and I make decisions based on what I can see, while I always hope and pray for the best and for God's grace." Grant debated whether he should say what next came into his mind. He decided to do so. "Besides, when we first met, I got the impression that you assumed the worst about me."

Bryant sat quietly, presumably listening to the exchange between the two men.

"Perhaps. But I was aware of your background in the U.S. military and with the CIA," declared Borget.

"And you assume the worst about the U.S., correct?"

"That is more than assuming."

Grant again shook his head. "Well, then, it sounds like you and Mr. Bryant are working from the same ... assumptions."

Bryant remained expressionless.

Borget said, "So, is Mr. Bryant here evil?"

Grant answered, "It's quite evident that he broke the law. He broke an oath, not just to his country, but to his family. And his actions resulted in the deaths of at least three dozen individuals – some who were doing what they could to counter evil, and some were children."

Borget paused, and then asked, "But is he not forgiven?"

"If he truly repents, I will be happy to hear his confession. But the forgiveness offered through Jesus Christ does not wipe away the consequences of his action in this life."

Borget said, "And that brings us back to the question of whether or not he has something to confess. I remain unclear as to whether or not what you said was true or not. I grant that it has given me pause. But perhaps in his view, Mr. Bryant was doing what he thought was right."

'That's very relativistic of you, Father Charles."

Chapter 22

While Grant and Borget engaged in discussion, two SUVs arrived in the middle of the small Village de Saint Paul. The main road and few small offshoot streets were otherwise quiet.

Four men exited each vehicle, and began scouring the area.

The only business with lights on was a small bar. Russell Leach entered with two of his French teammates. Leach remained inside the door, as the two Frenchmen circulated amidst the 14 or so people enjoying drinks and conversation. They asked if anyone had seen anything out of the ordinary during the day, claiming that a few friends might be in danger.

Most of the people watched the men skeptically, and said that they had not seen anything.

However, a fat man with a thick mustache sitting by himself waved over the two men. He said, "Yes, I saw something strange. A large vehicle arrived in town. It was parked just down the road, and I saw three men – two who were very strong – enter the monks' store. I did not think anything of it. After all, people show up here on a somewhat regular basis to purchase some of their chocolates." He took a sip of his drink, and then added, "You know, their chocolates are quite good."

The two men nodded in response.

The fat, mustached man continued, "As I was saying, I did not think anything of it, and went back to my business. Sometime later, I happened to glance out the window once more, and I see one of the monks get into this large car. And he drives it away. Very odd."

One of Bellanger's men asked, "Is that it?"

The man shrugged, and simply said, "Yes." He returned to his drink.

Leach and his two men left the bar, gathered the rest of their team, and went to the monastery's store. They broke in, and started to survey all parts of the establishment.

As much as Father Ron, Brother Al and Father Jules had tried to be thorough in their cleaning up after the two shot bodies earlier in the day, there was only so much time.

Traces of blood quickly became evident to members of the Bellanger team.

One of Leach's men returned to the bar, and moved across the room to the fat man. He simply asked, "Where do the monks live?"

The man smiled and laughed. "Where do they live? Just keep following the road. You cannot possibly miss the Monastere de Saint Paul."

That generated laughs from others, as the member of the team led by Marvin Blade and Russell Leach left the building and climbed into the waiting SUVs.

Chapter 23

After the Learjet landed at Avignon Airport, a small van was waiting for Sean McEnany and Chase Axelrod – again courtesy of another one of Tank Hoard's CIA assets.

McEnany drove, while Axelrod took stock of the supplies provided.

After Axelrod climbed into the front passenger seat, McEnany asked, "Are we good?"

Axelrod replied, "More than adequate for our purposes."

McEnany nodded, and said, "Try Stephen's number again, and the hardlines for the monastery and the store."

"Stephen warned that there was no service, and no one would be answering in the store."

McEnany replied, "Yeah, I know."

Axelrod dutifully went through calling each number, as he had done a couple of times during the flight. When he was done, Axelrod simply observed, "Still nothing."

McEnany observed, "The lack of anyone picking up at the monastery bothers me."

They drove on in silence for a few minutes, and then Axelrod said, "Stephen is thinking the same way that we are in terms of Bellanger possibly sending people looking for Bryant. He's either moved the monks and whoever else is there out of the monastery, or at least secured them somehow. That also means he is prepping to deal with possible hostiles."

The two men were basically repeating a conversation that they had had on the plane earlier.

McEnany increased his already rapid driving speed. He commented, "I'm not losing anyone else due to Hunter Bryant or Garth Bellanger."

Axelrod replied, "I'm with you."

Chapter 24

Pastor Stephen Grant's debate with Father Charles Borget had continued.

But after listening in silence, Bryant interrupted and started repeating much of what he had said during the Paris press conference with Garth Bellanger. Anger was evident in his voice and eyes. "I'm ashamed that I worked at the CIA. But I did learn things. I learned that the real threat in the world was the United States government. America plays games, stomps around the world like a big child, and the results are deadly. Innocent lives are lost..."

Wow. Is this guy working off of a sheet of talking points?

Grant interrupted, "Who did you lose, Bryant?"

"What?"

"Who did you lose? It's clear that this is intensely personal for you, and I think it's more than just a misguided allegiance to a twisted version of transparency or freedom. Who was it? What happened?"

Bryant's anger managed to intensify. "Yes, I lost someone. A person who was becoming ... who was ... important to me. And that person is dead, and it's all because of the U.S. being where it shouldn't be."

Grant took a stab. "Did she serve in the military?"

"Yes, damnit!"

Grant repeated, "What happened?"

Bryant's expression of anger immediately gave way to a distant gaze. He stared up at the stars emerging in the sky. "I met her, Lucy, on a blind date. We had a great time. And we went on two more dates. Then she had to return to her post in South Korea. She was an MP. She seemed to appreciate my joke that I liked a woman in uniform." He smiled sadly, but Bryant's gaze remained far off. "We exchanged a few email messages, and then they just stopped. I knew she wouldn't just stop answering me. She couldn't. And then I found out what happened..." He lowered his head. "She died in a car accident in Seoul, South Korea. A car accident. It made no sense. And, and, I knew we were supposed to be together. But now that wasn't possible."

He turned on his country and his family, and sent innocent people to their deaths, because a woman he went out with on a few dates died in a car accident?

Borget said, "I'm very sorry, my son."

My son? This isn't a mea culpa. It's not being sorry for what he did. And it's not a request for forgiveness. It's him justifying his horrible...

Grant's thoughts were interrupted by two sets of headlights emerging from the trees on the road below. He moved to a crouch to get a better view.

Crap. I'm pretty sure Sean and Chase didn't take separate rides.

"Bryant, I think your friends have arrived." He grabbed a roll of duct tape that was among his supplies, and he moved to Bryant. He placed his gun down while starting to pull off a strip of the tape. In the corner of his eye, Grant saw Borget rising to his feet.

Grant said to Bryant, "Stay still." As he put the tape over his captive's mouth, Stephen added to Borget, "Father, you need to sit down, please."

Grant started to turn his head toward a sound that Borget had made. But he never saw the butt of a semiautomatic rifle speeding at him.

Borget's swinging of the rifle came with notable force. Grant was knocked off his feet. His head struck the short wall of the turret.

While his head swam, Grant heard Borget say, "God, forgive me."

Borget turned the rifle around, and pointed it at Grant. He then said to Bryant, "Go, get out of here. Leave with those people down there so we will not have any more violence."

The vehicles stopped on the road in front of the church.

Bryant froze in surprise. But then he tore off the duct tape with his still bound hands, and picked up the gun Grant had put down.

Borget looked at Bryant, and said, "No, no. Your people are here. You do not need the gun. Just go down the stairs and leave."

But it became apparent that Bryant wasn't listening to the monk. He stood up and stared at Grant who was on the ground rubbing his head. Bryant smiled and started to raise the gun.

Borget again said, "No, please go."

Bryant took a step toward Grant.

Borget then turned the rifle and pointed it at Bryant. "Please go."

Bryant took another step forward.

Borget stepped backward, but declared, "I will not let you shoot him."

Bryant looked at Borget, and said, "Oh, really, Father?"

Grant started to say, "Please, don't..."

Bryant pointed the gun at Borget.

Grant summoned all of his strength and tried to gain some degree of balance that would allow him to get to Bryant.

Bryant pulled the trigger.

Father Charles Borget wore a look of surprise and horror, as the force of the gunshot sent him back and over the short wall. The monk was silent as he fell. But his body made a gruesome thud and crunching sound when striking the ground in front of the eight members of the Bellanger team.

After he pulled the trigger, Bryant began to turn toward Grant. But Stephen already was in motion. He managed to gain some thrust, and drove himself into Bryant's midsection. Grant wrapped his arms around the man, and pushed forward. Bryant dropped the gun, and began to fall back as well. As Bryant's body hit the floor, his head also struck the wall.

Chapter 25

On top of the north tower, the sound of the gunshot obviously drew the attention of both Father Ron McDermott and Brother Al McClay. The two men saw Borget tumble over the side of the south tower and plummet to the ground.

Brother Al yelled, "No!"

Ron blessed himself, and said, "Dear God."

McClay looked down at the eight men on the ground. He shouted, "You bastards!"

That declaration led to Bellanger's team firing up at Brother Al and Ron.

McClay picked up one of the handguns distributed earlier by Grant and McDermott. He looked at Ron, and declared, "We have to act."

The firing below stopped as the shooters had no clear look at their targets.

McDermott, who was positioned low and up against the turret wall, started to reply, "Okay, let's think about..."

Brother Al interrupted, "Grab a gun and come on. Follow me." He turned toward the door.

Ron replied, "No, Al, that's not the plan."

"Yeah, well, the plan also didn't include Father Charles being shot and falling to his death."

"Of course not, but..."

McClay once again cut off Ron. "You can come or not. But I'm going down there." He reached to unlock the door leading inside the tower.

"Al, the point of coming up here was that we'd have the high ground, and be able to..."

McClay unlocked the door, and swung it open. As he started to move through the doorway, he said, "The hell with the high ground."

As he watched Brother Al go through the door, McDermott said to himself, "Shit. Where the hell is General John Buford when you need him?"

As he looked around at the weapons lying before him, McDermott kept mumbling, "The high ground, the high ground," in a voice impersonating Sam Elliott.

Chapter 26

On the ground, Marvin Blade gave out orders. One man was to remain by the SUVs. He ordered two others to scour the rest of the buildings and grounds of the monastery.

Four others, including Russell Leach, were to follow him inside the church. He declared, "They're using the towers to their advantage."

After entering the church building, Blade pointed Leach and another man to the north tower, and he took the two others with him and moved toward the entrance to the south tower.

* * *

Grant's head was still spinning, though not as badly as earlier, as he pushed himself away from Bryant. He reached up and felt blood trickling from the wound on the side of his head thanks to Borget.

I'm sorry that your being naïve cost you so dearly, Father Charles. He felt a stab of guilt. *Too harsh, Grant?*

Stephen focused his vision on the closed eyes of Hunter Bryant.

Dead or unconscious?

Grant put off that question, grabbed a rifle, and half staggered, half crawled to the door. He pulled it open and crawled through the archway onto the shaky, circular stairs that ran down to the bottom of the tower. He leaned over the edge of the stairs to look down, which made his head swim even more.

The tower was lit only by shafts of moonlight coming through a few windows, and by light coming from the church via the open door at the bottom.

Grant's attempt to look down was met with rising gunfire from Blade and his two men.

Grant pulled back, clumsily moved his rifle, and pointed it down at his opponents. He began to squeeze off return fire, but as his vision bounced around, Grant had no idea if his shots were even coming close.

However, the same could not be said of the rounds coming at him. One slug ripped into his already bloodied monk's robe, and penetrated his upper right arm.

Grant struggled to not scream out in pain. He managed to get off some return fire, but now he had even less control over his aim.

*   *   *

A similar exchange of fire was taking place in the north tower. Through no fault of his own, Brother Al didn't make it too far down the stairs before Leach and his partner entered below.

Ron had decided to follow Brother Al through the tower doorway.

Now, McClay and McDermott were exchanging fire with the two men below. They had maintained the high ground.

But at the same time, the refurbished north tower stairs were wider and offered greater cover for Leach and his partner.

*   *   *

What are your options, Grant? Your head and arm aren't cooperating, and are only going to get worse.

He fired off additional shots in response to continued gunfire from below. Grant then looked over his shoulder and through the doorway.

One option?

He breathed in deeply several times, and fired off several rounds. Grant then put aside the rifle, managed to get to his feet, and staggered through the doorway. He looked at Bryant, who was still unmoving. And then Grant heard shots coming from the north tower.

Crap. Ron. God, please be with him.

Grant lunged at his target. He grabbed the handle of the case, and worked to focus on dragging himself and the case back to the stairs.

He fell through the door, and the case slid toward the edge of the stairs. Grant held his breath as the container stopped before dropping over the edge.

He crawled forward, and pulled the case back. Grant then grabbed the rifle once more, and fired off a wave of shots down toward the Bellanger team.

With the return fire, Grant actually prayed that his opponents had remained on the ground or only a few steps above it.

He snapped open the case to reveal nine grenades. Grant didn't pause. He concentrated, seized the first grenade, pulled the key, and dropped it over the side. He quickly did that two more times, and started to push himself back from the edge of the stairs.

Hopefully, this won't bring down the entire tower.

Marvin Blade had made it up eight steps on the stairs, and he was the first to recognize what was descending toward him. He turned and started to jump down toward the doorway leading out of the tower. He began to yell. "Get the..."

But the first grenade passed him by, struck the floor and exploded.

Blade's body was redirected against the thick stone wall of the tower, as were his two partners. The subsequent two grenades finished the job. The explosive force ripped apart the three men, and destroyed the lower twenty feet of the old stairs. While the 11th century stone walls of the church shook, they suffered mere superficial wounds.

Grant was sprawled on the floor of the turret waiting for something more to happen.

Apparently, 11th century monks knew what they were doing on the construction front.

Grant could hear gunfire in the north tower mixing with the sound of falling water just to his south.

Necessity and adrenaline allowed Grant to focus, and to rise to his feet.

He picked up the handgun that Bryant had shot Father Charles with, loaded a new magazine, and shoved it into the pocket of his robe.

Grant then seized a rope that had been included in the supplies from the SUV. He looked over the side to see one of Bellanger's men standing by two SUVs. Grant tied one end of the long rope around a stone prong in the turret, and the other end around his waist. The pain in his right arm made that a considerable accomplishment. But that would be nothing compared to what he was about to attempt in an effort to save his friend, Ron, and Brother Al.

Grant quietly slipped over the side of the turret, tightly gripping the rope in his left hand. His right arm would be useless as he tried to support his weight while lowering himself down the side of the stone church tower.

As he proceeded, the gunfire from the north tower continued to ring out.

Three thoughts kept running through his mind as he slowly descended.

First, as he looked down at Bellanger's man, Grant thought, *Don't look up.*

Next was to himself, *Faster, Grant, faster.*

And finally, *Dear Lord, please help.*

Nearly halfway down the side of the 70-foot tower, Grant knew that the man on the ground would look up. Stephen managed to stop the descent with the grip of his left hand, and against excruciating pain, reached inside the pocket of his robe with his right. He pulled out the gun.

The sounds of shots from the north tower didn't distract Grant, but instead made him focus even more. He aimed the gun. The man looked up, and began to move his weapon.

Grant pulled the trigger.

The projectile smashed into the man's skull, and he fell to the ground.

Grant let the gun fall to the ground, and he slid more quickly down the rope, burning and scraping his left hand while doing so. His legs took the impact of hitting the ground, but the rest of his body crumpled.

Grant heard more shots, so he got up once more, and grabbed the dead man's semiautomatic rifle.

Moving as quickly as he could, Grant staggered through the monastery gate and into the church. He focused his unsteady vision on the entrance to the north tower. When he arrived at the door, Grant didn't stop. He went through looking up for a target. He found one, and fortunately, it was a clear shot. He took it, and the man fell back against the stone wall.

Further up the circular staircase, Russell Leach leaned out to see what had happened. He turned his rifle on Grant, but shots from above, from the guns of both McClay and McDermott, descended into Leach's body. Russell Leach fell forward and dropped some 20 feet to the floor.

Grant then turned and moved back into the nave of the church.

The last two of Bellanger's team had entered at the other end, and were moving toward him with guns pointed.

Stephen could no longer move his right arm, and his head now spun worse than ever before. He dropped the gun and lost his balance. Grant fell sideways, but managed to grab hold of one of the church's simple pews. He wound up in a sitting position on the floor, leaning his left side against the bench.

Lord, if this is it, please watch over Jen.

Grant then heard a familiar voice in the distance. "You have one second to drop your guns, or you will die."

Sean?

The two assailants paused, and then complied.

As McEnany and Axelrod swept in to secure the two men, McEnany called out, "What's the situation, Stephen?"

He worked to call back. "With these two, I think that's it."

"Where are the others?" asked McEnany.

Grant breathed in deeply. "Ron and Brother Al are in the north tower."

The two Bellanger men were immobilized – with hands and feet zip tied.

Ron and Brother Al came into the church from the tower.

McEnany then asked, "What about Bryant?"

Grant said, "Shit. Right. I left him on the turret of the south tower. Not sure if he's dead or unconscious."

McEnany looked at Chase, and said, "Get Grant out to the van. Start patching him up. I'll get Bryant."

Chase replied, "Sean?"

McEnany had already turned away and was heading toward the entrance to the south tower. He said, "Just do it."

Grant said, "Sean, the stairs are rubble. I don't think you can get up there."

McEnany continued walking, and said in a voice that no one else could hear, "Oh, I'll get up there."

McEnany went through the doorway, and paused. He looked at the wreckage and then looked up. McEnany then stepped forward, and began climbing up the debris.

Chapter 27

Ron and Brother Al slowly and carefully helped Stephen out of the building and to the van driven by McEnany and Axelrod. They opened the back doors, and Grant sat down on the back of the vehicle.

After Axelrod had dragged the first of his prisoners out of the building and deposited him against one of the SUVs in clear view of McDermott and McClay, he asked, "Did you find the medical kit?"

McDermott answered, "Yes, and Brother Al brought out some of what the monks have in their infirmary."

Al and Ron were working to clean and bandage Stephen.

Al remarked, "You're lucky that the gunshot went through clean, and avoided hitting anything major."

Grant replied, "I think this is the part where I say: Yeah, thanks, it feels great." He paused, and continued, "Thanks, guys. You were amazing through all of this."

McDermott said, "Us? You're kidding, right? Tell me, Mr. Bond, if the stairs in the south tower are wrecked, then how the hell did you get to the entrance of the north tower to save us?"

Grant merely smiled, and then grimaced, as Brother Al worked further on the head wound. Al said, "I'm part of what we call a medical team here at the monastery. As I look at these injuries, I can probably sew you up, you know, if you're not interested in heading to a hospital?"

Grant nodded. He then looked back and forth at the two men. "Are you okay with having to do what you did?"

Brother Al said, "Unfortunately, I had to shoot someone once on the job." He left it at that.

Grant looked at Ron.

McDermott said, "I'm guessing that once this is over, it's going to sink in, and I'm going to feel terrible about it all. And then the healing will start."

Brother Al nodded, and Grant said, "Like I've said before, you are a wise man."

"Besides," added Ron, "I'm going to have one heck of a story to hold over Tom's head."

With that reference to their mutual friend, Tom Stone, Stephen smiled.

Axelrod returned with his second prisoner. As he placed him next to the first, a gunshot rang out from atop the south tower. Everyone looked up helplessly.

Grant waited for a signal from McEnany that he was alright.

Just a few seconds later, he saw a body come over the side of the turret, and begin a rapid descent.

Dear Lord, no.

Grant immediately recognized the clothes. Hunter Bryant landed face first, just a few steps from the body of Father Charles.

Chapter 28

About fifteen minutes after Hunter Bryant fell to his death, Sean McEnany managed to climb back down the stairs and the debris in the south tower of the monastery church. He exited the church, passed through the monastery gate, and then all eyes fell upon him.

He walked over to Grant, and they were joined by Axelrod.

Grant merely said, "Well?"

McEnany looked back and forth at Axelrod and Grant. He said, "By the time, I got up there, Bryant had managed to get loose. He fired a shot at me and, fortunately, missed. I got in close. We fought. And, well, he went over the side." He glanced over at the two bodies at the bottom of the south tower, which were now covered with blankets.

Axelrod merely replied, "Okay."

Grant watched McEnany.

I can never tell what he's thinking. Is he lying? Would he lie to me? He would if it meant protecting Chase and me, not to mention Rachel and the family.

Axelrod said, "Brother Al is going to take me to the hardline phone, and I'll call Paige."

McEnany said, "I'll come with you. I have to reach a contact in the DGSI." Sean was referring to France's General Directorate for Internal Security.

Grant said, "Sean, can you hold up a second?"

"Sure." He looked at Axelrod, and said, "I'll be right behind you." After Axelrod walked away, McEnany said,

"So, are you worried about me, or am I supposed to be worried about you, given your head and arm?"

Grant said, "Brother Al and Ron have these wounds under control, and Al's going to sew me up in the infirmary shortly."

"Right. Good. What else?"

"I'm both your friend and your pastor. You can tell me anything, and it's always between us."

"I know that, Stephen."

"Don't take this the wrong way. I'm just reminding you that I'm available for private confession, if you need it."

"Confession? Are you kidding? I'm not sure what I'd confess."

Is this the right time for this?

Grant decided to continue. "On more than one occasion in recent years, I've wrestled with something I've done that lies far beyond the usual duties of a pastor – to say the least. Indeed, that's the case with some actions I took relating to Bryant. You wonder about regret and the reality that you might just do it again under the same or similar circumstances. But..."

Sean looked directly into Stephen's eyes, and asked, "Do you think I lied about what happened between Bryant and me on that church tower?"

Grant paused, and then said, "I try to operate under the rule that whatever my family and friends tell me is the truth. At the same time, I worked in the world of espionage, and I understand the need to protect people. I also understand the desire, feeling the need, to act due to a sense of justice, or even revenge. I've been there. But I also understand that there's the regret..."

McEnany interrupted, "No, you don't understand. It's not that I just don't regret it, or that I'd do it again reluctantly in a similar situation. I'm not wrestling or wondering. In reality, Stephen, I would do what I did on that tower, again." McEnany looked over at the covered body of Hunter Bryant. "In fact, I wish I could do it again."

Grant went silent.

McEnany turned back to Grant, and asked, "We good?"

Grant nodded, and added, "If you need to talk, I'm here for you always."

McEnany slapped Grant on his good shoulder, and said, "I know. Thanks."

*   *   *

McEnany's call led to a team from the DGSI arriving on the scene within an hour. They spoke to everyone, and took control of the two survivors from Bellanger's team. The duo turned out to be rather chatty when a deal involving their freedom was dangled in exchange for information regarding Garth Bellanger's involvement in this and more.

A short woman with black hair and dark eyes was standing with McEnany, watching assorted activity. She said, "Thanks for the call, Sean, and for all you did here."

McEnany replied, "I appreciate you handling this, Camille."

She looked around, and summed up, "My team is taking Bellanger's people, the dead and the living, their vehicles and equipment. The monks will take care of their abbot, and you get to take Bryant's body back to the U.S. You're sure about your people getting here?"

"Yes, they landed about an hour ago, so they should arrive shortly."

"Good. As long as no one gives us any shit, we'll be arresting Bellanger tomorrow."

"Do you really see it happening?"

"Even with politicians, there's just too much evidence and carnage now. It'll happen."

"Good."

Camille added, "If not, I'll know who to call." She smiled and extended her hand.

McEnany shook her hand, adding, "Well, you have my number. I'd be happy to give the phrase 'Free Garth' a very different meaning."

*   *   *

After being sewed up by Brother Al, Grant slowly wandered into the monastery church by himself. He thought about kneeling down in front of the altar, but wasn't sure if his current wounds would allow him to get back up. So, he merely sat down on the first bench.

He looked up at the cross hanging above the altar, and breathed in deeply. Grant then folded his hands and bowed his head.

Dear Jesus, where do I start? I'm not sure if I could have or should have done something different. I put it all at your feet, and rely in the end fully and completely on what You have done for me, for all mankind. I ask for forgiveness, and thank you for your love and sacrifice.

And please be with Sean. Guide and comfort him.

I pray the same for Ron, Brother Al, Father Jules, and everyone else here at Saint Paul's. Be with them all, and help everyone through the death of Father Charles.

In addition, I ask that you watch over Paige, Charlie, and others with CDM traveling here.

Grant heard one of the church doors open and close. He continued praying.

And thank you, dear Jesus, for being with me throughout, and for allowing me to return to Jennifer and the people at St. Mary's. Amen.

Grant blessed himself, stood up and turned in the direction of the door that had been opened.

Paige Caldwell took a couple of steps forward from the shadows, but she stopped after getting a full view of Grant. The side of his head was bandaged, and he was still wearing the bloody robe. "Oh, my, Stephen, are you okay?"

Grant smiled slightly, and said, "Yeah, I'll survive. It's good to see you, Paige."

The two stood nearly 20 feet apart. She continued, "Are you sure you're alright?"

Grant nodded, "Yes. One of the monks here did a nice job patching me up."

"Well, in that case..." She pulled out her phone, pointed it at Grant, and snapped off a few pictures.

"What was that for?"

"Needed a shot of the warrior monk." She now was smiling gleefully.

"You called me that before."

"Yes, and I sent you a gift as well. You just need the sword."

Following the first time Paige and Stephen worked together after being long separated from their CIA days, Paige sent him a Christmas gift. It was a painting of a knight of the Crusades, battered and bloodied by battle, and wearing a soiled and torn tunic with a red cross on a white background. The knight held a sword firmly, and a light radiated from behind. He also had green eyes and black hair, like Stephen.

That is a nice painting.

"Jennifer has an assortment of swords." Grant's wife had an extensive sword and dagger collection.

Paige paused. Her smile persisted, but it might have faded ever so slightly. She said, "Yes, I know, and I'll send her these photos once I get somewhere with cell service."

"Just make sure you don't send them until I've completely brought her up to speed, and assured her that I'm okay. She's still a civilian and my wife."

"Have you spoken with her yet?"

"Briefly on the monks' phone."

"Yeah, these guys need to get some cell service."

"I don't think it's a priority."

"Maybe it should be, given what just happened."

Grant shrugged in response.

"Chase and Charlie are loading Bryant's body into our van. Are you and Ron returning home with us? We're leaving here in 15 minutes, at the latest."

"That's good. Brother Al got a hold of Father Jules. The monks and their guests are on the way back."

Paige commented, "You handled this brilliantly, Stephen."

"I'm not so sure about that."

Caldwell folded her arms, and said, "I know of no one else who could have done it."

Grant ignored that comment, and said, "As for Ron and I, we discussed it with Brother Al. We're going to stay and help with Father Charles' funeral. And then we'll head back to the states."

"Okay. Do you want to come outside and say goodbye to Sean, Chase and Charlie? Brooke and Kent are with me, too."

"Of course. But one more thing. Keep an eye on Sean, and let me know if there's anything out of the ordinary."

"Sure. I assume you have the same doubts about his Bryant story that I have?"

He answered Caldwell's question with a silent stare.

She smiled, and said, "Yeah, yeah, you're a pastor. You're supposed to trust people."

That's what Father Charles basically said.

Caldwell continued, "I'll play the cynical, suspicious spy."

"It's a matter of understanding each person."

She said, "How diplomatic."

"Well, that's something I've learned is needed at times as a pastor."

She shook her head, and said, "Okay. Let's go. I assume the guy that repelled down a church tower with the use of one arm doesn't need any help."

While walking slowly, Grant replied, "I certainly do not. But thanks, anyway."

Epilogue

A few days later, Pastor Stephen Grant exited a store. He opened the front passenger door of the Renault Scenic, and said, "Well, it's all in the hands of Fedex now."

Father Ron McDermott responded, "Thanks for sending my packages of the monks' chocolate as well. We can straighten out what I owe you on the plane home."

"Sounds good."

The two men were on their way to the Charles de Gaulle Airport, where they were supposed to return the rental car and board a flight for home. After the Hunter Bryant incident at the Monastere de Saint Paul and the funeral of Father Charles Borget, McDermott and Grant left earlier than what was originally planned. Grant also canceled meetings for the Lutheran Response to Christian Persecution that he had scheduled for after their stay in the monastery.

The time at the monastery was supposed to be about reflection and relaxation. It had turned out very different, and Grant now found himself feeling more at ease as Ron drove toward the airport.

Grant leaned his head back and closed his eyes. He said, "Thanks again for driving, Ron."

"More than happy to get behind the wheel."

A mere minute of silence passed when Grant's smartphone rumbled. He picked it up, and looked at the screen.

Blocked number?

He answered, "Hello."

"Pastor Stephen Grant?"

I know this voice?

"Yes, who is this?"

"Stephen, I am so glad I reached you. When we worked together, you knew me as Cardinal Juan Santos."

Grant sat up straighter, and said, "Pope Paul, how are you?"

After the death of Pope Augustine, Cardinal Santos had been elected pope, and became Pope Paul VII.

Ron whipped his head and raised an eyebrow. He silently mouthed, "Pope Paul VII?"

Grant nodded.

Pope Paul replied, "I am not well, Stephen."

"What is it? Can I help?"

"I think you might be the only person who can help. However, I cannot talk to you about this over the phone, nor do I have time right now to fully explain. But I need you to understand that this truly is an emergency, and it not only involves the future of the Church, but..." He paused.

"Yes?"

"One person has died, and I believe that more lives hang in the balance."

"Juan..." – *Juan?* – "...what can I do?"

"I understand you are in France? That is what Pastor Charmichael told me."

"Yes."

"Can I impose upon you to come to Rome?"

"Now?"

"I apologize, Stephen, but yes, can you come immediately?"

The pope of the Roman Catholic Church sounds desperate, and is seeking my help.

"Of course, I happen to be on my way to the airport now. I'll simply change my flight, and head to Rome."

"Thank you, Stephen."

Grant could hear some minor relief in the pope's voice.

Pope Paul VII added, "When you receive my text, just follow the instructions on where to go."

"Yes, of course."

"May the Lord be with you, Stephen. I look forward to seeing you soon."

Before Grant could respond, the pope ended the call.

McDermott looked over at Grant, and asked, "What the heck was that all about? Why is Pope Paul VII calling you?"

"He was grave and cryptic. The pope said that he needed to see me immediately, and that the future of the Church and lives were in the balance."

Ron managed to only say, "Wow." After several seconds of silence, he asked, "What now?"

Grant looked at his friend, and said, "I'm changing flights, and heading to Rome. Care to come along? I'm sure your boss won't mind."

Acknowledgments

Once again, thank you to the members of the Pastor Stephen Grant Fellowship for their support:

<u>Ultimate Readers</u>
Jody Baran

<u>Bronze Readers</u>
Michelle Behl
Tyrel Bramwell
Gregory Brown
Mike Eagle
Sue Kreft
Gary Wright

<u>Readers</u>
Robert Rosenberg

I appreciate Beth for so much, including her love, edits and support. I also treasure and am very proud of my two sons, David and Jonathan.

I, once again, thank The Reverend Tyrel Bramwell for his generosity and talents in creating the cover for this book. Please check out his books as well.

Any and all shortcomings in my books are all about me, and no one else.

As always, I take great encouragement from the fact that so many readers find some enjoyment in my books. And as long as someone keeps reading, I'll keep writing. God bless.

Ray Keating
November 2019

About the Author

This is Ray Keating's twelfth entry in the Pastor Stephen Grant series. The first nine novels are *Warrior Monk*, followed by *Root of All Evil?*, *An Advent for Religious Liberty*, *The River*, *Murderer's Row*, *Wine Into Water*, *Lionhearts*, *Reagan Country*, and *Deep Rough*, along with the short stories *Heroes and Villains* and *Shifting Sands*. A second edition of *Warrior Monk*, with a new Author Introduction and a new Epilogue, was published in early 2019.

Keating also is an author of various nonfiction books, an economist, and a podcaster. Among his most recent nonfiction books are *Free Trade Rocks! 10 Points on International Trade Everyone Should Know* and *The Disney Planner 2020: The TO DO List Solution*. In addition, he is the editor/publisher/columnist for DisneyBizJournal.com. Keating was a columnist with RealClearMarkets.com, and a former weekly columnist for *Newsday*, *Long Island Business News*, and the *New York City Tribune*. His work has appeared in a wide range of additional periodicals, including *The New York Times*, *The Wall Street Journal*, *The Washington Post*, *New York Post*, Los Angeles *Daily News*, *The Boston Globe*, *National Review*, *The Washington Times*, *Investor's Business Daily*, New York *Daily News*, *Detroit Free Press*, *Chicago Tribune*, *Providence Journal Bulletin*, *TheHill.com*, *Touchstone* magazine, *Townhall.com*, *Newsmax*, and *Cincinnati Enquirer*. Keating lives on Long Island with his family.

Enjoy All of the Pastor Stephen Grant Adventures!

Paperbacks and Kindle versions at Amazon.com

Signed books at raykeatingonline.com

• *Deep Rough: A Pastor Stephen Grant Novel* by Ray Keating

One man faces challenges as a pastor in China. His son has become a breakout phenom in the world of professional golf. The Chinese government is displeased with both, and their lives are in danger. Stephen Grant – a onetime Navy SEAL, former CIA operative and current pastor – has a history with the communist Chinese, while also claiming a pretty solid golf game. His unique experience and skills unexpectedly put him alongside old friends; at some of golf's biggest tournaments as a caddy and bodyguard; and in the middle of an international struggle over Christian persecution, a mission of revenge, and a battle between good and evil.

• *Shifting Sands: A Pastor Stephen Grant Short Story* by Ray Keating

Beach volleyball is about fun, sun and sand. But when a big-time tournament arrives on a pier in New York City, danger and international intrigue are added to the mix. Stephen Grant, a former Navy SEAL, onetime CIA operative, and current pastor, is on the scene with his wife, friends and former CIA colleagues. While battles on the volleyball court play out, deadly struggles between good and evil are engaged on and off the sand.

• *Heroes and Villains: A Pastor Stephen Grant Short Story* by Ray Keating

As a onetime Navy SEAL, a former CIA operative and a pastor, many people call Stephen Grant a hero. At various times defending the Christian Church and the United States over the years, he has journeyed across the nation and around the world. But now Grant finds himself in an entirely unfamiliar setting – a comic book, science fiction and fantasy convention. But he still joins forces with a unique set of heroes in an attempt to foil a villainous plot against one of the all-time great comic book writers and artists.

• *Reagan Country: A Pastor Stephen Grant Novel* by Ray Keating

Could President Ronald Reagan's influence reach into the former "evil empire"? The media refers to a businessman on the rise as "Russia's Reagan." Unfortunately, others seek a return to the old ways, longing for Russia's former "greatness." The dispute becomes deadly. Conflict stretches from the Reagan Presidential Library in California to the White House to a Russian Orthodox monastery to the

Kremlin. Stephen Grant, pastor at St. Mary's Lutheran Church on Long Island, a former Navy SEAL and onetime CIA operative, stands at the center of the tumult.

• *Lionhearts: A Pastor Stephen Grant Novel* by **Ray Keating**

War has arrived on American soil, with Islamic terrorists using new tactics. Few are safe, including Christians, politicians, and the media. Pastor Stephen Grant taps into his past with the Navy SEALS and the CIA to help wage a war of flesh and blood, ideas, history, and beliefs. This is about defending both the U.S. and Christianity.

• *Wine Into Water: A Pastor Stephen Grant Novel* by **Ray Keating**

Blood, wine, sin, justice and forgiveness... Who knew the wine business could be so sordid and violent? That's what happens when it's infiltrated by counterfeiters. A pastor, once a Navy SEAL and CIA operative, is pulled into action to help unravel a mystery involving fake wine, murder and revenge. Stephen Grant is called to take on evil, while staying rooted in his life as a pastor.

• *Murderer's Row: A Pastor Stephen Grant Novel* by **Ray Keating**

How do rescuing a Christian family from the clutches of Islamic terrorists, minor league baseball in New York, a string of grisly murders, sordid politics, and a pastor, who once was a Navy SEAL and CIA operative, tie together? *Murderer's Row* is the fifth Pastor Stephen Grant novel, and Keating serves up fascinating characters, gripping adventure, and a tangled murder mystery, along with faith, politics, humor, and, yes, baseball.

• *The River: A Pastor Stephen Grant Novel* by Ray Keating

Some refer to Las Vegas as Sin City. But the sins being committed in *The River* are not what one might typically expect. Rather, it's about murder. Stephen Grant once used lethal skills for the Navy SEALs and the CIA. Now, years later, he's a pastor. How does this man of action and faith react when his wife is kidnapped, a deep mystery must be untangled, and both allies and suspects from his CIA days arrive on the scene? How far can Grant go – or will he go – to save the woman he loves? Will he seek justice or revenge, and can he tell the difference any longer?

• *An Advent for Religious Liberty: A Pastor Stephen Grant Novel* by Ray Keating

Advent and Christmas approach. It's supposed to be a special season for Christians. But it's different this time in New York City. Religious liberty is under assault. The Catholic Church has been called a "hate group." And it's the newly elected mayor of New York City who has set off this religious and political firestorm. Some people react with prayer – others with violence and murder. Stephen Grant, former CIA operative turned pastor, faces deadly challenges during what becomes known as "An Advent for Religious Liberty." Grant works with the cardinal who leads the Archdiocese of New York, the FBI, current friends, and former CIA colleagues to fight for religious liberty, and against dangers both spiritual and physical.

• *Root of All Evil? A Pastor Stephen Grant Novel* by **Ray Keating**

Do God, politics and money mix? In *Root of All Evil?*, the combination can turn out quite deadly. Keating introduced readers to Stephen Grant, a former CIA operative and current parish pastor, in the fun and highly praised *Warrior Monk*. Now, Grant is back in *Root of All Evil?* It's a breathtaking thriller involving drug traffickers, politicians, the CIA and FBI, a shadowy foreign regime, the Church, and money. Charity, envy and greed are on display. Throughout, action runs high.

• *Warrior Monk: A Pastor Stephen Grant Novel* by **Ray Keating**

Warrior Monk revolves around a former CIA assassin, Stephen Grant, who has lived a far different, relatively quiet life as a parish pastor in recent years. However, a shooting at his church, a historic papal proposal, and threats to the pope's life mean that Grant's former and current lives collide. Grant must tap the varied skills learned as a government agent, a theologian and a pastor not only to protect the pope, but also to feel his way through a minefield of personal challenges. The second edition of *Warrior Monk* includes a new Introduction by Ray Keating, as well as a new Epilogue that points to an upcoming Pastor Stephen Grant novel.

All of the Pastor Stephen Grant novels are available at Amazon.com and signed books at www.raykeatingonline.com.

Join Ray Keating's Email List

If you join Ray Keating's Email List, you'll receive Pastor Stephen Grant stuff, including a regular newsletter, special savings, various updates, and assorted contests and giveaways!

Join now by quickly filling out the contact information at

http://www.pastorstephengrant.com/contact.html

Join the Pastor Stephen Grant Fellowship!

Visit
www.patreon.com/pastorstephengrantfellowship

Consider joining the Pastor Stephen Grant Fellowship to enjoy more of Pastor Stephen Grant and the related novels, receive new short stories, enjoy special thanks, gain access to even more content, receive fun gifts, and perhaps even have a character named after you, a friend or a loved one.

Ray Keating declares, "I've always said that I'll keep writing as long as someone wants to read what I write. Thanks to reader support from this Patreon effort, I will be able to pen more Pastor Stephen Grant and related novels, while also generating short stories, reader guides, and other fun material. At various levels of support, you can become an essential part of making this happen, while getting to read everything that is written before the rest of the world, and earning other exclusive benefits – some that are pretty darn cool!"

Readers can join at various levels...

• **Reader Level at $4.99 per month...**

You receive all new novels FREE and earlier than the rest of the world, and you get FREE exclusive, early reads of new Pastor Stephen Grant short stories throughout the year. In addition, your name is included in a special "Thank You" section in forthcoming novels, and you gain access to the private Pastor Stephen Grant Fellowship Facebook page, which includes daily journal entries from Pastor Stephen

Grant, insights from other characters, regular recipes from Grillin' with the Monks, periodic videos and Q&A's with Ray Keating, and more!

- **Bronze Reader Level at $9.99 per month...**

All the benefits from the above level, plus you receive two special gift boxes throughout the year with fun and exclusive Pastor Stephen Grant merchandise.

- **Silver Reader Level at $22.99 per month...**

All the benefits from the above levels, plus you receive two additional (for a total of four) special gift boxes throughout the year with fun and exclusive Pastor Stephen Grant merchandise, and you get a signed, personalized (signed to you or the person of your choice as a gift) Pastor Stephen Grant novel three times a year.

- **Gold Reader Level at $39.99 per month...**

All the benefits from the above levels, plus your name or the name of someone you choose to be used for a character in one upcoming novel.

- **Ultimate Reader Level at $49.99 per month...**

All the benefits from the above levels, plus your name or the name of someone you choose (in addition to the one named under the Gold level!) to be used for a major recurring character in upcoming novels.

Visit
www.patreon.com/pastorstephengrantfellowship

Enjoy

Free Trade Rocks! 10 Points on International Trade Everyone Should Know

by Ray Keating

Paperback and for the Kindle at Amazon.com

Signed books at raykeatingonline.com

While free trade has come under attack, Ray Keating lays out in clear, simple fashion the benefits of free trade and the ills of protectionism in *Free Trade Rocks! 10 Points on International Trade Everyone Should Know.*

Tapping into his experiences as an economist, policy analyst, newspaper and online columnist, entrepreneur, and college professor, who taught MBA courses on international business and entrepreneurship, Keating explores and explains in straightforward fashion 10 key points or areas that everyone - from entrepreneurs and executives to students and employees to politicians and taxpayers - needs to understand about how trade works and how free trade generates benefits for people throughout the nation, around the world, and across income levels.

The 10 points or areas covered in *Free Trade Rocks!* are...

Point 1: Do People "Get It" on Free Trade?
Point 2: Economics 101 on Trade
Point 3: Debunking Trade Myths
Point 4: Trade and the U.S. Economy
Point 5: Trading Partners
Point 6: Trade and Small Business
Point 7: Ills of Protectionism
Point 8: Brief History of Free Trade Deals
Point 9: The Morality of Free Trade
Point 10: The Future of Trade

Keating makes clear that nations don't trade. Instead, businesses and individuals trade, and free trade is simply about expanding the freedom to trade by reducing or eliminating governmental costs and restrictions.

Regarding *Free Trade Rocks!,* Dan Mitchell, Chairman of the Center for Freedom and Prosperity, declares, "A common-sense explanation of why politicians and bureaucrats shouldn't throw sand in the gears of global trade."

And Self-Publishing Review gives *Free Trade Rocks!* four stars, and says: "International trade policy has come to the forefront of global politics, making *Free Trade Rocks! 10 Points on International Trade Everyone Should Know* by Ray Keating a timely and fascinating read for a suddenly curious demographic. Keating manages to bring this seemingly dull subject to accessible life with real-world examples often torn straight from recent headlines, along with a comprehensive and (mostly) impartial view on the topic. As the exclamatory title suggests, Keating is a fan of free trade, but his deep expertise spanning a wide range of subjects and career paths makes this book an engaging, informative, and essential read for those who want to weigh in on this hot-button issue."

Also, George Leef, the Director of Research at the James G. Martin Center for Academic Renewal, observes, "Ever since Donald Trump started talking about foreign trade, I have thought that what the country needs is a clear, easily understood book that explains why the government should not mess with free trade. Lo and behold, Ray Keating has written exactly that book. *Free Trade Rocks!* clears away the myths and misconceptions that trade interventionists count on."

Check Out Ray Keating's "TO DO List Solution" Planners

Available at Amazon.com and at raykeatingonline.com

Ray Keating's TO DO LIST SOLUTION planners combine a simple, powerful system for getting things done with encouragement and enjoyment on a daily basis.

Books scheduled for publication late in 2019 include:

• *The Pastor Stephen Grant Novels Planner 2020: The TO DO List Solution*
• *The Disney Planner 2020: The TO DO List Solution*
• *The Lutheran Planner 2020: The TO DO List Solution*

Get more information about these and other nonfiction books from Ray Keating – along with special savings – by joining his email list.

Go to https://raykeatingonline.com/contact

Visit DisneyBizJournal.com

News, Analysis and Reviews of the Disney Entertainment Business!

DisneyBizJournal.com is a media site providing news, information and analysis for anyone who has an interest in the Walt Disney Company, and its assorted ventures, operations, and history. Fans (Disney, Pixar, Marvel, Star Wars, Indiana Jones, and more), investors, entrepreneurs, executives, teachers, professors and students will find valuable information, analysis, and commentary in its pages.

DisneyBizJournal.com is run by Ray Keating, who has experience as a newspaper and online columnist, economist, business teacher and speaker, novelist, movie and book reviewer, podcaster, and more.

Tune in to Ray Keating's Podcasts

Ray Keating's Authors and Entrepreneurs Podcast

This entertaining podcast is geared toward readers, aspiring authors, entrepreneurs, and aspiring entrepreneurs. It explores the world of authors as entrepreneurs. The podcast discusses the creative and business aspects of being a writer, and what that means for authors themselves as well as for the reading public. Keating serves up assorted insights and ideas.

Listen in and subscribe at iTunes, or on Buzzsprout at http://www.buzzsprout.com/147907

Free Enterprise in Three Minutes Podcast

This podcast provides three-minute (give or take a few seconds) answers to important questions about free enterprise, the economy, business and related issues. Ray Keating cuts through the economic mumbo-jumbo, tosses aside the economic mistakes often made in the media and in political circles, and quickly gets at economic reality. Who says free enterprise and economics have to be mind-numbing? That's not the case with Free Enterprise in Three Minutes with Ray Keating.

Listen in and subscribe at iTunes, or on Buzzsprout at http://www.buzzsprout.com/155969

Enjoy
"Chuck" vs. the Business World: Business Tips on TV by Ray Keating

Paperbacks and for the Kindle at Amazon.com

Signed books at raykeatingonline.com

Among Ray Keating's nonfiction books is *"Chuck" vs. the Business World: Business Tips on TV*. In this book, Keating finds career advice, and lessons on managing or owning a business in a fun, fascinating and unexpected place, that is, in the television show *Chuck*.

Keating shows that TV spies and nerds can provide insights and guidelines on managing workers, customer relations, leadership, technology, hiring and firing people, and balancing work and personal life. Larry Kudlow of CNBC says, "Ray Keating has taken the very funny television series *Chuck*, and derived some valuable lessons and insights for your career and business."

If you love *Chuck*, you'll love this book. And even if you never watched *Chuck*, the book lays out clear examples and quick lessons from which you can reap rewards.

Ray Keating's Services for Authors and Entrepreneurs

• **A Business Plan – An Action Plan – for Your Book**
Ray Keating will read your manuscript and provide a personalized, 12-point business plan for your book. That plan will cover such areas as

• identifying your market;
• ideas for using social media to promote your book and interact with readers;
• a personalized media release for your book created by Ray Keating;
• suggested advertising options based on various budgets;
• specific actions you can take for working with the media;
• identifying a variety of promotional tools that fit with your book;
• steps for identifying speaking opportunities;
• and more, depending on the specifics of your book.

This is a plan of action for your book – a roadmap for you to follow.

If you're an author, then you are an entrepreneur. That's the message Ray Keating communicates in his Authors and Entrepreneurs Podcast and to fellow writers, and it's the reality that he executes with each of his own books. As an author and entrepreneur, you need a business plan – that is, an action plan – for your book. That's where Ray Keating is able to help fellow authors on an individualized basis.

While most authors enjoy writing their book, many are unsure about the business aspects of being an author. Specifically, they're uncertain about or uncomfortable with what's needed to get their books into the marketplace, that is, into the hands of readers. Ray Keating's personalized business plan for your book offers a roadmap to assist you, the author, in becoming a better entrepreneur when it comes to your book.

We know what authors do. They, of course, write. But what's an entrepreneur? An entrepreneur both owns and operates a business. Entrepreneurs are not passive shareholders. They're not managers for someone else who is the owner. Entrepreneurs both own and actively run their businesses. That's also what authors do. Creating a book is very much like launching a startup business. Authors' creations are their products. And no matter whom authors work with, authors own their books. Their books, in effect, are their businesses.

Ray Keating notes, "My impression is that most writers don't like the business end of things. But if an author is serious about setting and reaching sales goals, no matter how big or small, then every author needs to embrace the role of the entrepreneur. Entrepreneurs own and operate their own businesses. That's exactly what authors do. Your books are your passion, your creations and your business. You are the owner and operator of your books, if you will, and you need to work for their success. You need a business plan for your book."

Whether you are going the route of traditional or indie publishing, you need a business plan – an action plan – for your book.

Visit raykeatingonline.com and click on "Ray Keating's Services for Authors and Entrepreneurs"

• **Manuscript Assessment and Feedback on Your Book**

Ray Keating will read your book, and provide an "Assessment and Feedback" memo that offers thorough thoughts and suggestions, such as on story, plot, characters, dialogue, clarity, consistency and structure. Throughout his career in writing, business and teaching, Keating has always appreciated constructive feedback for his own efforts, and believes that such feedback is critical for authors and entrepreneurs. Ray Keating's "Assessment and Feedback" service focuses on the complete book, pointing out the positives and suggested areas for improvement.

Visit raykeatingonline.com and click on "Ray Keating's Services for Authors and Entrepreneurs"

• **Copyediting for Your Book**

Perhaps your book simply needs a quality round of copyediting. Ray Keating offers that service as well. The copyedit will not touch the content of your book, but instead will focus on issues like spelling, punctuation, grammar, terminology, and capitalization, along with matters of continuity when it comes to plot and characters. This is especially critical for authors who plan to take the indie or self-publishing path.

Visit raykeatingonline.com and click on "Ray Keating's Services for Authors and Entrepreneurs"

Made in the USA
Columbia, SC
02 October 2021